A House on the Piazza

Prose Series 36

KENNY MAROTTA

A HOUSE ON THE PIAZZA

GUERNICA
Toronto·Buffalo·Lancaster (UK)
1998

Antonio D'Alfonso, Editor.
Guernica Editions Inc.
P.O. Box 117, Station P, Toronto (ON), Canada M5S 2S6
250 Sonwil Drive, Buffalo, N.Y. 14225 U.S.A.
Gazelle, Falcon House, Queen Square, Lancaster LR1 1RN U.K.

Legal Deposit — Fourth Quarter
National Library of Canada
Library of Congress Catalog Card Number: 95-75426

Canadian Cataloguing in Publication Data
Marotta Kenny
A house on the piazza
(Prose series ; 36)
ISBN 1-55071-032-X
I. Title. II. Series.
PS3563.A6795H68   1998   813'.54   C95-900172-7

Table of Contents

To the memory of my father

A Seamstress

A week before the wedding, the bride's sister awoke to find the bride blue in the face beside her in bed. From that moment, the wailing didn't cease. The two old ladies, Zia Lucia and Zia Rita, saw to that, and the godparents were sent for to add to the clamor. But Filomena, the seamstress, didn't see what Donna Maruzza was grieving about. (The family had brought her in to sew the trousseau, since their own fingers were too fine for the task.) Donna Maruzza had had only the two daughters left to marry, and now that the older was dead, of course the younger would have the other's intended, and the rich woman could sleep all day if she wanted. Was that why she mourned? Did she wish she had the luck of Filomena, who could rejoice in six daughters still unmarried, with no money, no prospects, and no brother to defend them?

But the family didn't bother to explain themselves to Filomena. By the time they remembered she was there, the table was already piled high with food the visitors had brought. It was more food than Filomena's daughters would see in a month, though they could make it disappear in an hour; being single didn't lessen their appetites. Donna Maruzza's son came out to Filomena, who was by then at her regular place, at her machine outside the front door. The house was on the piazza, and from her bench Filomena could see the people walk by as she worked.

Nino looked more solemn than usual, and he usually looked as if his sister had just died. All the same, he had not lost the expression all young men wore when addressing Filomena, an expression that said, "Pardon my formality, but enjoy it, too; for you'll never know me at closer range."

"Here's your pay," said Nino, holding out his hand. Filomena counted the coins with her eyes.

"What's that?" she asked.

"Your pay," Nino repeated.

"But it's less than half what you owe me," Filomena observed. "And I've almost finished the clothes."

"My sister no longer needs your clothes," said Nino. "I'll take you home in my cart."

"Forgive me," said Filomena, "but I can't take less than my work is worth."

"Truly," said Nino.

"You'll need the clothes for the younger girl, won't you?"

"I don't know what the custom in your family may be, *Signora*, but in ours we don't prepare the wedding of one daughter when her sister is lying dead. You might as well take this money. Possibly we'll consider hiring you again when the time comes for another wedding."

"Possibly?" Filomena asked, her eyes wide.

"Possibly," Nino repeated in cold blood.

"And what if there isn't another wedding?" Filomena inquired. "Now that God has given the boy a second chance, maybe he'll come to his senses?"

"Thank you for your concern, *Signora*," said Nino, "but in our family the daughters don't have to beg in the street for husbands."

"Because they can buy them in the market?" Filomena asked, but Nino didn't reply.

"All right," Filomena went on, "in that case, I'll take the clothes I've finished instead of my pay. Your sister, should she find a man, will no doubt want a finer seamstress than myself; and your mother will be able to pay her with the money she's saved today."

"If you don't take what I've offered, *Signora*, you'll leave with nothing at all," said Nino.

"Not the trousseau? Not my pay?"

Nino jerked his head upward, meaning "no," after each question.

"Well, then, if I must," said Filomena, and she pushed away the hand held out to her, rejecting his money. Nino puffed himself up like a rooster. "I'll send for my husband to take me home. May I wait here until he comes in his cart?"

"You may wait here until you rot, *Signora*," said Nino, and he walked back inside.

Sitting alone outside the house, Filomena naturally spoke to the visitors arriving with their condolences. And if she was going to speak at all, how could she keep back the way Donna Maruzza had cheated her, with her own daughter lying dead in the house? Filomena admitted that she shouldn't complain about having been cheated, for she had no one but herself to blame, in accepting work from such a woman. She was wrong to have expected everyone to be as honest as herself and every woman to respect her daughters as Filomena respected her own. "After all," Filomena said, "Donna Maruzza will no doubt tell you that flesh and blood pass like water, but gold lasts forever."

"No, Filomena," they assured her. "The gold Donna Maruzza gets this way will turn to ashes in her hand. Don't let her rob you, Filomena," they advised.

But Filomena insisted that being robbed was less painful to her than seeing so wealthy a family disgrace itself. And it was the groom Filomena felt most sorry for, she said. When he arrived and saw the people gathered around the seamstress, he naturally joined the group to see what was wrong. He was a fine-looking young man, though his eyes were red with grief. He wore a thick mustache, with long spikes at the end — full enough to have served for a hairpiece.

Filomena tried to reassure him. "Myself, I've never believed that you marry a family's reputation in marrying its daughter," she said. "And I'm sure you don't believe it either, or you wouldn't have betrothed yourself to the child of a woman like Donna Maruzza, am I right?"

"But what's happened?" the boy asked.

"So what if she tries to profit from her daughter's death?" asked Filomena. "So what if her daughter's honor isn't worth enough in her eyes for Donna Maruzza to keep the contract she made with me? You shouldn't let this trouble you, you're marrying the sister now, the family says, and I'm sure they value her honor at least as much as they valued your bride's. And after all, don't riches excuse all things?"

When they told the groom the details of how the family had denied Filomena her pay, he threw his cap on the ground. (So much does honor mean to the young.) Filomena tried to calm him, telling him she would rather give up her pay than have a spot rest on the departed spirit of his former bride-to-be, but he refused to be calmed. He put his hand on top of Filomena's black sewing machine, as solemnly as if it were the stone on his mother's grave, and said, "I'll see that you're paid." Then he went into Donna Maruzza's house.

They could hear him, even through the shutters, which had been properly closed since dawn, and above the wailing, for the two old ladies were no match for his strong young voice. They could hear Nino's voice, too, and a new cry, which must be Donna Maruzza. Was she pleading with him to leave his money behind? For the next thing they knew, the young man had stalked back out of the house. His departure raised new shouts inside, and other mourners followed him out, returning to their homes without waiting for the funeral. Even the dead girl's godparents brushed past Filomena's machine, the loving godfather, and the godmother, who had found the fine groom that Donna Maruzza had now so foolishly lost.

By the time the priest arrived, few mourners were left except the old women, who naturally expected a gift in return for their labors. As he approached the door, Filomena stopped him to ask his blessing; and as he made the sign of the cross, she told him what had happened. But the learned man went inside all the same. You had to have six unmarried daughters to know for what it was the value of prayer. And it helped if your daughters were like Filomena's: like Rosalia, pretty enough but with a sickness that put her to sleep if she sat still more than two minutes at a time; like Lucia, so clumsy with the fingers remaining to her, and Pasqualina, who couldn't count past one; like Pia, who combined the worst of all her sisters, and was the oldest as well, so that she naturally expected to be married first. Such daughters instructed you in God's love for his children.

Was Donna Maruzza waiting to see if Christ Himself would come, in the absence of other mourners, to attend the funeral, or was the priest only waiting until she offered a big enough bribe? For it was a long while before the wailing quieted and the priest's chanting began. But at last Filomena heard the sound of the funeral through the shutters.

Then some note of the priest's reminded Filomena of one of the songs she often sang to accompany her work, and it inspired her to begin hemming a sheet while she sang. An unmarried girl wouldn't have sung it, but there was no harm in it for an old married woman like Filomena. The song was about a foolish girl who went to the fields to collect greens for her mother and found more help than she expected. It was a good song for working, because there were so many stanzas, you'd think it never ended.

But Filomena came nowhere near the end. Hardly had she begun before Nino was standing in front of her again.

"I thought my tongue would have to be separated from my body before it would speak to you again," he said. "But Donna Maruzza, a widow as well as a bereaved mother, has asked me to ask you to let my sister receive the last rites from God."

"Am I stopping them?" Filomena asked, with an expression of surprise.

"I won't deny that I tried to talk her out of it, but my mother has asked me to tell you that you can have the part of the trousseau you've finished if you'll keep quiet until the funeral is over."

"For a song, she'll pay what she wouldn't for my sweat, and for her own word?" Filomena asked.

"She's offered you what you want," said Nino. "What more can you ask for?"

This was a question worth thinking about. While Filomena pondered it, she asked him another. "Tell me this: your sister's groom will be sorry he's missing her funeral. Where do you suppose he's gone?"

"To hell, I presume," Nino replied.

"To seek his bride, do you think?"

"I'm surprised you don't know his intentions, *Signora*, as friendly as the two of you are."

"Friendly? I haven't heard him ask for my daughter's hand."

"That only proves that he's a man, *Signora*," said Nino, "not that he isn't your friend."

Then Filomena thought of the answer to his question. "Tell your mother," she said, "that I'm willing to take what she offers, if she'll add a little something for my wasted morning."

"A little something? And what's that?"

"Not much," said Filomena. "Only a husband."

"A husband," Nino repeated. "Don't you have a husband? The whole town thought it was one of God's miracles, like the parting of the sea."

"Ah, Nino, a mother never thinks of herself. I mean a husband for one of my daughters."

"Filomena, not even the devil could find a man to marry your daughters."

"You're too modest, *Signore*. I'm sure you can find a protector for one of my girls. You need to find a husband for your own sister now, don't you? While you're looking for one, just look for two. And I'll tell you this: so confident am I of your abilities, I'm going to accept your mother's offer, and take a little relaxation from my work."

With that, Filomena took the sheet from under her needle, folded it, returned it to her basket, and closed her hands on her lap.

Nino looked at her. "I don't know what's in your mind, Filomena."

"Go," she said, "pray for your sister's salvation. After all, anything is possible."

So Nino went inside, and Filomena sat idle. She looked at the houses on the piazza, deciding which she would live in if she were rich. She shooed away a chicken that became too curious about the finished blouses and undergarments and bedding she had piled in her basket. She nodded to several women who passed by, bringing food out to the men in the fields. She asked a child to bring her some water from the fountain, since she didn't want to leave her post; it's not so easy to accustom yourself to leisure and freedom when you've had a life of work and servitude. And in the background all the time was the sound of the priest's voice.

Then the door opened, and the family emerged. Donna Maruzza, supported by her daughter, was hidden in a shawl, her body bent over halfway to the ground. Filomena tried to get her attention, to convey her sympathy, but not once did the mother or daughter seem to notice her. Nino, on the other hand, never took his eyes off Filomena, even as he and the priest, for want of other men, lifted the coffin into Nino's cart. He watched

Filomena as if a harmless old woman could kick out like a donkey or strike like a snake. Even as he walked off with the cart to the churchyard, followed by Zia Rita and Zia Lucia — for Donna Maruzza was apparently too feeble to go with them — he cast more than one look back at Filomena. What wickedness was he imagining?

When he returned, he stopped the cart which had carried his sister's body and said to Filomena, "I'll take you home."

"No, thank you," said Filomena. "I'll wait here."

"So is that it?" Nino asked, rearing back. "Are you going to stay here for the rest of your life as our guest? I'm afraid you might find it inconvenient, since you won't be allowed in our door to sleep, or for any other reason."

"But lower your voice, Nino. Your mother looked quite weak to me, you shouldn't upset her," said Filomena. "I admit, I'll miss the opportunity to share my bed again, as I had to the last two nights in your house, with the donkey and the chickens. But in fact, I've sent for my husband, and I'll be leaving when he comes."

"In that case," said Nino, "I doubt I'll be speaking to you again — until I've found a husband for one of your daughters, of course. But it's just possible, you know, that your death will come first. Maybe the one who dozes will drop a candle and set fire to your bed, or the one you sometimes take along for your helper will step on the pedal of your machine when it's your neck under the needle, instead of one of her fingers. Since this might happen, let me say to you now that I hope God judges you as kindly as I do."

"I thank you for your good wishes," said Filomena, "and I sincerely wish you the same."

She didn't speak to Nino again for several days. He didn't visit her house nor did she go seeking him. The first day she had the time, she went to sell in the market, as she did on days when she had no work on her hands. Mostly it was eggs she sold, and occasionally an extra garment she had made from cloth she had spun and woven herself. But now she had almost a whole wardrobe to dispose of, and of the best fabric, too, as she assured buyers with her cries.

"Blouses! Petticoats!" she sang, planting herself before the closed shutters of Donna Maruzza's house. "Linen and silk, the finest work! Made for Donna Maruzza's daughter, who never wore them! Buy them from a poor woman, cheated and abused!"

She only made a few sales the first day, but this was partly her fault, since she passed up an offer to buy her entire stock. She hadn't been selling long that day when Nino came out of the shuttered house.

"So it's my mother's death you want, Filomena?" he asked.

"How kind of you to come out to see me," Filomena replied.

"Do you think I would be here if my mother, who barely has the strength to talk today, hadn't pleaded with me to come? What do you want?"

"But you know what I want," said Filomena.

"My mother is willing to throw her money away on something that already belongs to her," said Nino. "She says she'll buy whatever it is you're selling."

"How nice to have money," Filomena observed, "to be able to buy a trousseau you'll never need."

"Filomena, even if I could buy you a husband, you'd have five daughters left. What does one matter out of so many?"

"It would be a start," said Filomena. "But it wasn't my daughter I was thinking of, it was your sister. Have you been able to buy a husband for her? I haven't seen many young men visiting your family today, or many visitors at all, and that's surprising for a family in mourning, not to mention a lady who's ill. They all want to talk to me, though. Why should my word mean so much to them, do you think?"

But Nino offered no solution to this mystery, and Donna Maruzza had as few visitors the whole time of Filomena's selling. That was a number of days, for Filomena didn't have as much success at the market as she might have, and she was compelled to return again and again, until she had worn a rut in the dust before Donna Maruzza's house. Filomena liked to talk just as well, however, and she had told the truth to Nino: those who were hesitant to buy were very willing to take her story for free. After a while, there were few people who didn't know how Donna Maruzza had tried to pick Death's pocket, had dishonored her daughter by cheating the woman who had the sacred duty of making the virgin's trousseau. They had kept back Filomena's pay and then tried to placate her with part of the trousseau. Filomena had consented, of course, to avoid a scandal, but what use was a trousseau to her? Everyone knew the chances that her daughters, poor girls, would ever need one. Cash was what she had been promised, and cash was what was needed to keep her family from starving, from being buried alive by their debts. So what else could Filomena do but walk off her feet at market trying to make a few pennies from the clothes, worthless to her?

Some suggested she should demand of Donna Maruzza the original sum agreed upon. But Filomena asked them if they thought she would touch money now from such a family? The young men especially took up for her, naturally enough, since she'd done them a favor by informing them of the respect in which the family of Donna Maruzza held its daughters. And the boys knew she was only telling the truth and not speaking out of jealousy, since she so frankly admitted the limitations of her own daughters. After all, joke as people might about those poor girls, the bigger joke would now be on anyone so foolish as to marry Donna Maruzza's child.

On the rare occasions when Nino appeared in the piazza on some errand for his mother, he would be the object of much wit. When they spotted him with his donkey, they called out to ask if he was on his way to the madhouse in Palermo to find a brother-in-law.

The truth was sadder, they learned soon enough. It was medicines and doctors he was after, for his sick mother. And when these had failed, it became known that he had risked the shame of going to plead with the *fidanzato* of his dead sister; it was Donna Maruzza's wish that he would visit her once more. Everyone knew what that meant, for Donna Maruzza naturally could not leave an unmarried daughter behind her on earth. But the *fidanzato* rightly refused to come.

In the town's conversation, blame passed between Nino and Donna Maruzza. The father being dead, Nino was responsible for the family's decisions, some pointed out. But others answered that Nino was such a dutiful son, he acted only the will of his mother. Whoever was at fault, it was certain that the girl would not be showing her face again soon. If it was sickness that kept the mother home from church, it was shame that kept the daughter. "Thank God my own daughters don't know such shame," Filomena observed. The young men nodded, but they showed no more personal interest than if she had remarked that a diet of *cicidi* will give you gas.

Then, one evening — when everyone had gone home to prepare dinner, and Filomena herself was thinking of her hungry daughters, who couldn't have cooked a chicken if it had jumped into the pot — the door of Donna Maruzza's house opened behind the seamstress.

"Well, Nino!" she said when her old friend presented himself before her. "Have you come to invite me to your sister's wedding?"

"I've come to beg you to stop throwing dirt on our family," said Nino.

"I don't know what you mean," said Filomena, and she turned away from him.

"Forgive me, *Signora*," said Nino, touching her arm. "It's still possible you could tell people it was all a misunderstanding, isn't it? I don't believe you're a heartless woman. Think of my mother."

Filomena turned back. "Tell your mother," she said, "that I'm only selling what's mine."

"Filomena!" cried Nino.

"The poor must live, as well as the rich."

"Filomena!"

"I'd give her good health if I could, but that's only in the power of a just God. Now excuse me, *Signore*," she said, pushing him away with her basket, "I see another buyer."

"Filomena, tell me about your daughter Rosalia!" said Nino in one breath.

Filomena paused and looked at him. His fists were clenched and trembling, his eyes downcast, as is not unusual in young lovers. Filomena held out the basket to him, and he relieved her of her burden. Then the two of them began walking in the direction of her home.

"I have a better idea," said Filomena. "Let me tell you about my daughter Pia. She's my favorite."

Her Sister

"And why didn't we hear about these fits before?"

That was Enzo's mother's question when she heard the news.

"First a dowry a beggar would turn up his nose at — and now this!" The old lady flung out her hands, as if it were to spite her that her son's betrothed had died, mere days before the wedding.

Enzo himself, however, could think of nothing but some hasty words the girl had once spoken. Although the courtship had been brief — he had seen Assunta no more than a half dozen times, and always in the presence of her family — it had not been entirely smooth. One day, when he was telling her his plans, she suddenly opened her black eyes wide and said, "Then we're not going to America?"

Her surprise was understandable. The young men of Pianosanto had been going to America for over ten years, and the girls liked to follow them. For the single girls there was a larger field of marriageable men. Girls both single and married could find jobs there, at which they could earn their own money.

Enzo explained himself to Assunta, in the same terms he had several times offered to his mother. ("Is it to make sure your sisters die old maids?" Ma had demanded. "Is that why you want to stay in this pen that even the pigs have left behind?") In the low murmur that provided their only privacy, Enzo reminded the girl that most men went to America simply so they could come back and buy a house of their own. But Enzo was hampered by no such necessity.

His childless uncle Tonio, the lawyer, had promised him a house at the birth of his first son. Not just any house, either, but one of the noblest houses on the piazza, rumored to have once offered a night's rest to royalty. Like so many houses in Pianosanto, it had been empty for years. It had fallen into Zio Tonio's hands, the original owners having been distant connections of the family; but the lawyer preferred to live frugally, in the back of his office. The upright man, who wore a clean shirt and collar every day of his life, could think of no more fitting end for the house than once more to shelter the blood that had entertained kings.

Why go to America, Enzo asked his betrothed, to live among men who didn't know his name, when an abode suitable to his family's dignity already awaited him here? He and his wife would live with his mother until the moment came.

Ma had had an answer ready when he told her of it, of course; when had she ever had to go begging for words? Assunta, however, was properly silent for a moment after he confided his intention to her. And when she looked up from the hands folded in her lap, she smiled sweetly, as at an innocent child. Her teeth were small and perfect as factory-made *acini di pepe*. Nor was there any effrontery in the words she spoke at last, despite the disappointment they showed.

"You know," she said, "I've always planned to go to America. My cousin Mafalda has a job waiting for me."

"Ah, no," Enzo gently replied, making free to touch her wrist since her mother was engaged in conversation with Zio Tonio.

The girl seized back her arm, and stood up so quickly her chair scraped on the brick floor. "I'm going to America," she said, not loudly, but with an iron firmness that drew the attention of all. Her teeth were now bared in a less ingratiating expression. "If it's the last thing I do!" she added, and walked out of the room.

There had been nothing for Enzo but to leave as well. In choosing Assunta he had followed his uncle's counsel, as always: he had taken a girl without much money, and therefore sure to be deferential. Pa's mistake, Zio Tonio frequently observed, was marrying a woman with a little land of her own. To her poverty, Assunta added the charm of a good upbringing, for her family had been well enough off until quite recently, and still lived in a house on the piazza, not far from Zio Tonio's. Even now some townsmen were fooled by Donna Maruzza's manners, but Enzo's uncle had told him the facts.

Could Zio Tonio have made a mistake? So Enzo had asked himself after that scene at Assunta's. As to the money, Enzo's uncle must have been right, for Enzo himself had observed the meager life within the walls of Donna Maruzza's house. Was the mere memory of former wealth, perhaps, sufficient to induce a dangerous freedom in the girl's behavior? Or had Enzo been wrong to allow himself a girl of Assunta's striking beauty? He had thought that single gift could make little difference, given her limited means. But this show of pride!

Assunta's sin had been quickly atoned for, however. The next day Donna Maruzza had come to apologize (quite a journey for the old lady, in her frail state of health) and to assure him he would find Assunta changed if he returned. When he did the family this honor, though the girl was a little tight-lipped — and though her mother's troubled gaze never left her, as if Assunta were a pot that might at any moment boil over and douse the flame — she made no further objections. As the day approached, Enzo almost forgot about his uncle's house in his wonder that this fine creature was about to be his.

Now she belonged only to death — the daughter had proved frailer than the mother — and Enzo could not help thinking again of the girl's bold words. "The last thing I'll do!" It was as if she had thoughtlessly called her death upon her.

Two months passed before he could think of marriage again. When he did, it was only natural his thoughts should turn to the same family. They had grown no richer in the meantime; indeed, the story was that they'd tried to avoid paying for the girl's very shroud. And the brother himself had come, deferentially enough, to remind Enzo that there was another sister remaining.

The day Enzo went to meet Rosaria — she had always been there, but how could he see her with Assunta in the room? — he knew at once that she, at least, was unlikely to become guilty of even a moment's pride. Although not repulsive, she had none of Assunta's beauty. Her eyebrows grew together, as if permanently knitted in anxiety. Her face was drawn, possibly because, when not called upon to speak, she was always gnawing the insides of her lips, with a preoccupied look as if she were trying to remember the flavor she had once found there.

That wasn't all. Her family's manner with the girl revealed to Enzo, by contrast, how warily they had always treated Assunta. Indeed, Enzo felt it wouldn't have been improper if they had addressed Rosaria (or Saredda, as they called her) with a little more delicacy. Donna Maruzza spoke quite frankly of Saredda's luck in winning Enzo's interest, and did not endeavor to conceal her inferiority to Assunta in every respect. Nor did the praise of Assunta's greater piety, cleverness, and dignity seem to be only the poignant expression of so fresh a loss. Saredda appeared long practiced in acknowledging her sister's higher virtues.

Could a girl be too deferential? When Enzo first spoke of their wedding as a definite prospect, Saredda let out an inarticulate sound, like a gasp. And when he asked her thought, she replied, "Are you — are you sure you want to marry me, *Signore?*"

"Don't talk foolishness!" the mother scolded, her exertion bringing on a fit of coughing; and Enzo reassured the girl as he could. Still, throughout the courtship, Saredda, for all her efforts, could never sustain a smile longer than she could have walked on her hands. On the wedding day itself, still dressed in black, she looked more inconsolable than ever.

The secret came out at last, when the bride and groom sat receiving guests in Donna Maruzza's house, the trousseau hung up on strings for all to admire.

"*Signore,*" she began. She had not yet spoken his name to his face. She was trembling, and had evidently waited to speak until the view of the guests was cut off by one of her camisoles. "I must tell you. I'm afraid I have no right to — what should have been my sister's."

"What an idea!" Enzo replied with a smile. Her feelings must be strained by the sight of the linens and underthings; much of the trousseau was originally her sister's.

"It's Assunta, not me, you should be taking to America."

Enzo had been about to offer more reassurances when that word threw him off.

"America? But we're not going to America," he reminded her. Each time he spoke the name, she closed her eyes as a reformed voluptuary might at the glimpse of a naked limb. "I wasn't going to take your sister either. Did you forget?"

Saredda looked puzzled in her turn, but then said, with sad understanding, "Ah, that's right. It wasn't until after you were gone that she said it to my mother: how she didn't want to live in a house where people would say she didn't belong, to live even in a palace where, though she might be the king's wife, everyone would remind her she deserved no better than to be his servant. And she asked why Mafalda should get to wear a hat every day, and not her. But my mother said she must not think about America, but about keeping from starving — at least until she had the ring."

From her first sentence, Enzo had begun to stiffen and draw back in his chair. At her last, he positively froze. But Saredda didn't seem to notice.

"When you could no longer escape, my mother said, then she could surely have her way, for no man could ever deny her. And surely she would have. All the relatives, and my own godmother, too, used to kiss her and say that, even with her fits, she deserved to have been born a queen!"

"A queen in America?" Enzo said after a moment's silence. "And is that what you plan to be, too?"

If he had expected defiance, he was disappointed. Saredda only moaned, "As if just to think of it weren't crime enough!"

She had given him much to think of as well. Indeed, for a moment he had turned blood red, as if the color of his thoughts had dyed his face. But he was called to himself by the place, his *comare* just then walking in. Besides, Saredda's distress was evidently sincere. Her revelations might have come, after all, in quite another tone than her penitent one. Does the priest turn away even the blackest sinner, when he's coming for confession?

He glanced at the girl again. Her eyes were downcast with shame. "Rosaria," he whispered, so his approaching godmother wouldn't hear. He used the girl's formal name, as it had been used in the ceremony, to remind her of his pledge to her. "We won't speak more of this." He was beginning to think, after all, that he might have won the saintlier of the two sisters.

Certainly no saint could have accepted more humbly his mother's graceless welcome. The girl had hardly walked in the door before Ma was handing her the empty jug, so that the world might be granted the spectacle of a bride fetching water on her own wedding day. Enzo attempted to intervene. Didn't he have sisters who could go in her place? But Saredda insisted on taking the jug, like those virgin martyrs who didn't let their stigmata interfere with their lowly duties.

More than one of those martyrs, too, would doubtless have given Enzo the same answer he received from Saredda that night.

"Forgive me," Saredda said when he asked for an explanation. "Not — not yet."

He let her have her way, but he lost some sleep over it — among other reasons, because he wasn't entirely sure that his mother, with her penchant for the indecorous, might not insist upon displaying the sheet.

As it turned out, however, Ma had had no time to think of that, so busy had she been in devising chores for Saredda. She could begin with the dusting and sweeping; then she could take out the slops. Saredda did it all without complaint. Indeed, there seemed to be only one thing she objected to, and she made her objection three nights in a row.

On the fourth night, Enzo could no longer contain himself. "It will have to be some time, your fear will be the same until it's done, must we wait until we're dead?" He whispered, for his sisters were no further than the loft above, but his voice cracked on the last word.

"It isn't fear," Saredda replied, looking at the yoke of his nightshirt but doubtless not seeing even that. "It's — it's Assunta."

"Assunta?" She had spoken with such conviction, Enzo couldn't help glancing behind him.

"I know you said we shouldn't speak of it," the girl began, shaking her head in regret at her own misdeed.

"But when I put the pad on my head to carry the water, I always think of Assunta!"

It wasn't that Assunta had done it so often — as the younger sister, such chores ordinarily fell to Saredda — but Assunta never spilled a drop, never broke the jug, like her imperfect sister. Assunta's occasional stitching, too, it seemed, won universal praise; her once-a-year cooking had a taste as popular. What else could Saredda think of, when Enzo's mother sent her to the stove, or gave her some mending, but how much greater was Assunta's claim to the privileges Enzo offered — even if Assunta hadn't been his first choice as well?

"No one, no one would tell you different!" Saredda's whisper became a soft hiss. "It was for her my cousin Mafalda got a job, she never wrote a word about me. Mafalda's only been there a few years, you know," Saredda could not help interjecting, "and she already has three different pairs of shoes, ah!" She caught her breath, as if she had swallowed a fly.

"Let Mafalda keep all the jobs, let her be cut in two by the machine that would have done for your sister. As for you," Enzo added, reaching tenderly toward her, "what is your job but to be my wife? Would the priest have married us otherwise?"

She rolled away, making the straw in the mattress swish. "Do you think he'll be punished for it, too?" she asked, bringing a hand to her cheek as if she had a toothache.

Enzo heaved onto his back and said to the beams above, through which his sisters' snoring filtered down, "Maybe time will help."

The next morning he took his mother aside and asked that Saredda be excused from household tasks for the present.

The old lady didn't fly into a rage. She simply held out her hand and answered, "Three *lire* a week."

Enzo couldn't believe it. But all his mother would say was that if the girl wouldn't work for her board, then Enzo must pay. She reminded him that she had not yet seen a penny of what he earned from Zio Tonio; that she had fed, clothed, and sheltered him for ten years since he was old enough to make money; that she had daughters still to marry off, and a son who refused to make a home for them where that end might most naturally be achieved — that is, in America.

"Excuse me," Enzo replied solemnly, "I thought there was a matter of some blood between you and me. As for your daughters, I would have thought you'd rather have them wait, perhaps in a proper home, for husbands who are suited to them, rather than to run after those who are not."

His mother looked up at him: like his father he was a head taller than she. "So you're still thinking of that house your uncle holds in front of your nose, as he did with your cousin Luca before you?"

Enzo was shocked by the comparison, even coming from his mother. Luca had forfeited Zio Tonio's interest by marrying a woman so disreputable there was no telling what the origin of her children might be. "In this case," Enzo observed with a slight nod, "Zio Tonio doesn't have to fear any spot coming to his name."

"And if your uncle is so concerned about his name," the old lady replied, "why doesn't he give it to the child poor Nicolina, the peddler's daughter, bore him?"

This question always reminded Enzo that there was no use talking to her. It was a Saturday, and that night he turned over every bit of pay, leaving nothing even for a cup of coffee. Three *lire* was all he got for making himself available for Zio Tonio's extra copying. Then he looked at his wife. She sat just where he had left her that morning, in a position by which she evidently strove to take up as little room as possible.

"I hope you've been enjoying your leisure," he observed. "I'm paying enough for it." And when the time came, he couldn't even make his usual request, his stomach was tied up in such knots.

Nor, when his powers returned to him with the passing days, did Saredda's leisure appear to have produced all the effects he had hoped for. After a week, happening to pass through the piazza with his uncle, Enzo was conscious of some awkward feelings when the old man pointed to the wrought-iron balcony of the empty house.

"In a year," Zio Tonio said, nodding gravely, "you'll be sitting up there — if you've done what's right."

Enzo responded only by clearing his throat. There was no need to trouble his benefactor with the information that it might be rather more than a year before either of those events came to pass.

"I've been thinking," Zio Tonio went on; these deceptively modest words were always the preface to his advice. "Shame though it is to say, you may have had a lucky escape. A girl who looked like that Assunta, may she rest in peace, who can say what she might have led you to?" He clucked to himself. As a lawyer there was no crime he hadn't heard of, yet familiarity hadn't affected his principles. Whatever rumors were passed about his private life, it was well known that he wouldn't stay in a room where disgraceful jokes were being told.

"Your Rosaria," he concluded, "may have been the better bargain."

Again Enzo feigned assent. Tonio knew nothing of the weekly board, of course. Even if he'd considered Saredda a bargain at the price, however, Enzo might have observed that there was such a thing as false economy. As soon as she had been excused from chores — a release in which she took no pleasure — Saredda began to be plagued by dreams.

Dressed in her wedding clothes, the same that had served for her burial, Assunta rose up in the dreams to accuse Saredda of unpardonable presumption. Wasn't she ashamed to be waited on in her husband's house, as if his family were her servants? Didn't she know the world was appalled by her? Why, Assunta demanded, didn't Saredda start for America at once? She had as much right there, after all, to parade in a feathered hat and be bowed to the same as if she'd been somebody in Pianosanto, instead of the nobody she was.

"But no one thinks that of you!" Enzo assured his wife.

"If they don't, they should! My sister's right!" Saredda began to chew her knuckles.

Enzo took her hand from her mouth and held it between his own two. It turned cold at his touch, but this only added ardor to his words.

"How can you listen to that creature, a girl who wanted to defy her husband, to drag him where his name meant nothing? Besides," he added, as the haunted girl showed no sign of hearing anything but the terrible words of the dream, "what kind of woman could wish to cause such pain to a sister? How must she have been to you in life, to bring you such terror in death?"

This question succeeded in waking her: the look of fear was gone. But it was replaced by a gloomy wonder he recognized too well, as she took up one of her old explanations.

"But it couldn't have been wrong for Assunta to go there. Mafalda wrote us that they use only silk sheets in that country, and Zio Turiddu always said Assunta should sleep on nothing else. And she never did anything to me, even" — Saredda lowered her eyes a little in addressing this second point — "even when she pinched, or pulled my hair, she never did anything I didn't deserve."

Enzo couldn't speak, so far did these words go beyond his suspicion. When Saredda sought to withdraw her hand, he let it go lest she be reminded of her sister's torments. He looked at her hair, lying limply on the pillow. It was thin, not thick like Assunta's, who would probably not even have felt a yank.

As Saredda lay breathing beside him, in a world he was unable to rescue her from, Enzo could not help thinking of watching at his father's deathbed. But in body, at least, Saredda seemed healthy.

"Should we go to the priest?" he asked after a time. He had heard, in church, of possession by demons, the closest thing he knew of to Saredda's case.

The idea embarrassed her and, if truth be told, Enzo was relieved she shrank from exposing their private trouble. But it gave her a thought. Perhaps she could give a gift to San Rocco on his feast day, seeking forgiveness for her presumption — or, if that were too much, seeking only freedom. What she meant by freedom Enzo didn't ask, nor did he let himself think of how his father, in pain, had made the same prayer. Besides, Saredda's voice had brightened a little, as the sky does when the black clouds give place to gray ones.

Even so small a change was enough to make Enzo feel generous. "We could afford five *lire*, or six," he said; for he wasn't entirely without savings.

"Ah, you'd call six *lire* a gift, then," Saredda bleakly replied.

So the gift amounted to something more. When the *festa* came, not long after Enzo's talk with his uncle, the sum was enough not only to elate the priest, but to cause the band, who stopped at the houses of donors, to make its longest pause outside Enzo's mother's house. The stop was so long that no one could fail to notice. Certainly Ma herself didn't.

That evening, when the supper was through, she stepped into their corner and said to her son, "Well, then, what crime have you committed that required so great a gift? What crime that you'll confess to, that is, for I know how hardened you are about offenses to your flesh and blood."

As Enzo did not choose to reply, his mother went on.

"I'll admit, I was surprised to see this payment. I thought it was for that house you were saving the money you've stolen from my daughters."

"Ma — " Enzo began, tired already.

"But after all, I have only one thing to say to you. Since I see how rich you are, what I took three of before, I'll take five of now."

"Five!"

"Yes. Five, or the street." She gestured to the dirt path that unquestionably lay outside the door.

Enzo strode out and took that path, but only for the moment. He walked to the torchlit piazza where the explosions of the fireworks would seem like peace compared to the sound of women's voices. How could he pay? If he met her price, he'd soon enough have nothing, and Saredda's dowry as it was would hardly suffice to furnish a single room of the new house. He couldn't ask more of Zio Tonio. Whenever his father had admitted not standing up to Ma, Tonio would shake his head disgustedly, as at the confession of a murder or other impropriety.

Among the shadowy crowd he made out his uncle. Like everyone else, Zio Tonio had noted the band's serenade, and the generosity it signified.

"Enzo," he said, fixing his nephew with a curious gaze. "I hope it's no problem about the little ones?"

"No, Zio," Enzo replied, trying to keep all his thoughts from his face. "It was only to ask for holiness."

"Ah, I should have guessed." Then his uncle turned away. Enzo walked on, listening to those words over and over. Was there a new formality, a new distance in the old man's tone?

Back home, he didn't trust himself to look at Saredda, who sat as motionless in her best dress as if she were the decorated statue of San Rocco. He didn't speak to her until they were alone in bed. Then, although his turmoil would have made him useless for much, he turned to her and put his proposition once again. Had San Rocco heard her prayer?

"But — but it's so soon!" she stuttered, as if there were something to fear from him.

Certainly the look in his eyes would have given her reason. "Is it? Then we'll wait. And in the meantime you can take up this family's slops once more. My mother won't get five, she'll get none. And we'll stay in this house until my beard is gray!"

From that night on, he slept at his wife's side as little responsive to her presence as if she were a statue in fact. If she were anything else, if she knew a burning like her husband's, she was welcome to enjoy as he did the sensation of being eaten alive.

But after all, Enzo couldn't stay angry at Saredda, as the nights passed with no proof of San Rocco's intercession. She took up her burden of housework again with eager dutifulness, though it meant a return to still more burdensome thoughts. Enzo knew what she was feeling when, on hands and knees to scrub the bricks, she would suddenly pause, looking as if she'd found her doom inscribed there. Nor did her nights provide the rest she needed after her days of labor: her dreams, now that they had begun, refused to stop. How could he nurture bitterness when he saw her losing flesh? Her bedclothes were open to the collarbone, and he saw the strings of her neck grow prominent by the week.

Nor did Enzo dwell on his mother's crimes: what should have surprised him in her behavior? He knew where the greatest blame lay. He knew who had deluded him, lured him to his ruin. One day, returning from an errand to the next town in his uncle's cart, he stopped at the graveyard.

He hadn't visited since his wedding, months before. With the returning sun, shoots of wild wheat and asphodel covered her grave the same as others. Only the sharp edges of the stone distinguished it. The years of her life were pathetically brief; but they had proven long enough to do who knows what harm to him, to Saredda.

"Do you think to hide from me?" he demanded in his thoughts, looking at the stone. "Do you think from the protection of that earth you'll destroy us?"

His heart beat as if he had shouted out the words. And with the blood roaring in his ears, he solemnly resolved that, no matter how, he'd get a son and cheat the fate that seemed in store for him. "And may you be cursed!" he concluded, letting these last words find passage into the open air.

That night, by coincidence, Saredda spoke of a new idea. She told it as they lay in bed. This had come to be the place for conversation: free of his mother's commentary, Saredda would tell, in her hesitant, unassuming way, the little tales of her day; and he would repeat those happenings in the greater world he touched in his visits to Zio Tonio's office. It was as if they were old people together in the piazza, beyond everything but chatter, whose bodies are no more than blocks to drape the clothes on, whose flesh is as emptied of all promise as the chairs on which they sit. The couple never even spoke of her dreams any more. He knew she continued to have them only by her restlessness at night — and by this news of her plan.

"You know the feast of the Rosary is next week — my name day, you know."

He saw her thought at once. She had spoken with such modesty, however, that he tried not to scold as he informed her he could afford no more for the saints.

"No," she replied, "I think perhaps it was wrong to believe money was the answer. It might be something else the Virgin wants."

A meaner man, or one less given over to despair, might have turned these last words to blasphemy. Enzo only asked, with some weariness, what Saredda meant.

But it was a vow, and she could not tell him. She turned away, adding this to the other secrets she kept from him. Her mention of the subject, however, brought back all those thoughts of the impossible, and cost him another night's sleep.

When the town's spring *festa* arrived, Saredda was gone from the conjugal bed before anyone else was awake. Enzo's mother didn't remark on it, for no one could be expected to work on a feast day. When Enzo's sisters went out to watch the procession, he accompanied them. Saredda was sure to be following behind it.

They stood in the piazza looking east, where the Madonna of the Rosary was being carried between the shrine outside town and the church. All looked that way, as if they were the summer's wheat bending to the wind. Why should anyone have cast an eye the other way? True, processions had once included the western path as well, starting from the far edge of Cataldo's field, which lay like an apron on the side of a high hill, almost as straight up and down as if the apron were indeed hanging from a woman's waist. At the top of that hill an old stone crucifix was planted, worn with rain and kisses. But some years since, this walk had been found too tiring. It wasn't easy, especially if you wore pebbles in your shoes for penance, as the gravest sinners used to do, wearing hoods as well to hide their faces. It must have been in turning to slap a fly, or gossip with a neighbor, that someone happened to glimpse the western path and cried out, "Look there!"

Like the others, Enzo turned, saw nothing — then, yes, a spot. It moved slowly, and was strangely short. Was it a child? No, a woman on her hands and knees, her skirts bunched above. Had she really gone up the mountain and back again? Who could it be, they asked, though they would know soon enough, for she wore no hood. But Enzo was already running in the direction of the creeping penitent.

When he came close enough definitely to recognize her shape, he saw also that she was coated with dust, even her face, like a creature of mud. The coating was thicker on her forearms and her calves and feet: so thick that any cuts upon them, any blood, did not show, even when he was at her side.

"Saredda!" he cried. "What are you doing?"

She didn't reply, but went on, in a trance. Presumably silence was part of the pledge.

"But no one does this, Saredda! God Himself doesn't ask it!" Still she crept on; he could see her lungs heave.

"Saredda, come home!" he pleaded, kneeling to lift her up in his arms if necessary. But she resisted, moving on as relentlessly as Cataldo's threshing machine in autumn. Enzo walked beside her a little way, but it was like sitting at his father's bedside when he no longer recognized them, or even knew anyone was in the room. At last he began to walk at a normal pace back towards town, and then, uncontrollably, to run.

He stopped on the outskirts, however — stopped at the graveyard. Since his last visit, a blossoming weed had grown out of Assunta's resting place, a gaudy, heartless flower. He could have torn it from the ground, had he not had some last remnant of respect for what it touched. To prevent himself, he held his hands tightly in fists, until the white showed.

He opened his mouth, but there was nothing to say. He had already cursed her, and he couldn't expect her to answer his question, which was this: was it his life she held against him?

After all, however, he could answer this himself. It couldn't be his survival she begrudged him, for her enmity had begun before her death. If she had married him, it would have been only to thwart him. What was his crime in choosing her, that should have made her want to blight his life for all eternity, and the life of a sister, too, the blood of her blood? Ought not one sister to seek the other's good? And if she chanced to sin against it, ought she not be willing to give as much as her own life in atonement?

No response came to his unasked questions, not even a wind to disarrange the petals of the flower. He stood looking at it for a while, then returned to town.

His uncle was the first person he encountered. He was standing just outside the piazza. By now, everyone knew who was so slowly and painfully making her pilgrimage.

"Well!" Zio Tonio said, with no prefatory greeting. He had that flinty look Enzo had seen him wear only when debtors came into the office — and once, the peddler, poor Nicolina's father. "No wonder God has refused to bless you!"

Enzo was puzzled, but quickly answered. "Uncle, it's been only a matter of months!"

"Then pray that it's forever, as I do! To think of your shamelessness, bringing such a girl among us!"

"But what do you mean?" His uncle stepped back when Enzo put out a hand in appeal.

"I don't know what her crime may be, but the sight of that" — Zio Tonio pointed in the direction of Cataldo's field — "makes me afraid to ask."

He wouldn't listen to reason. Lest Enzo hadn't sufficiently understood, he stated explicitly that no penny of his would go to feed the offspring of a creature already guilty of such vice, at so young an age.

"My God, uncle, what shall I do?" Enzo cried. "Must I live forever in my mother's house?"

"Don't you have enough to take you to America with the other *cafoni*? Don't fear that you'll be missed!"

After that Enzo didn't know what he did. He bumped into the people crowded in the piazza without knowing who they were or what they said to him. For a time he carried a piece of fried dough a child had put into his hand. At last he was home, and Saredda was there, the Saredda of mud. She and his mother stood outside the doorway, Saredda in tears, mumbling to herself. When his mother spied him she said, "Now I see why you paid so much to bribe San Rocco! You thought you'd escape a disgrace like this!"

"But Ma!"

She didn't listen. "All I know," she said, "is that you have to get out. I have daughters to marry. You've taken enough from them without robbing their house of its reputation as well!"

A few weeks later, Enzo and his bride lay on a bed in a hotel near the docks of Palermo. It was still light, but they were tired from their journey, by cart, train, and streetcar. Above the stand with the ewer and basin hung tinted images of the king and queen, bidding a personal farewell. The hotel was full, and you could hear the sounds of many different families through the walls. All the same, it was more privacy than the couple had ever had. They might speak as loudly as they liked.

Yet they had said little. Saredda only repeated that he shouldn't have married her, she had no right to go where he was taking her. Enzo, when he could work up the strength, assured her it wasn't her fault, and besides — it was the coldest thing he was ever to say to her — there was nothing to be done about it now.

At the moment, Enzo was freed from the obligation of making any reply at all, for Saredda had been dozing since the dinner downstairs. He had noticed that she stirred in her sleep, as she did when she was dreaming. Indeed, when she suddenly woke, the first thing she said was, "Enzo, I've had another dream."

She placed her hand on his, no doubt frightened by the strangeness of the place. Enzo closed his hand around hers, but answered, "Please. It's time for sleep." Then he shut his eyes.

She heeded him and said no more. But then he felt her other hand on his shoulder. When he opened his eyes, she was looking straight at him. She blushed, but she looked, like an animal who has never seen a man before, and doesn't know whether to be afraid. Unlikely as it was, and with his own heart beating as in fear, Enzo guessed what she meant, and took her into his arms.

When they lay still once more, Enzo could not take his eyes off her. At last, when he could speak, he said, "But what did you dream?"

"I dreamed how — how I could rightly be your wife."

She was looking at him again, and the sight lifted Enzo to a kind of grave playfulness. "Do you think San Rocco will be waiting for you in America, then? Do you think you'll find the Madonna of your *paese* there?"

Saredda shook her head, then spoke in that familiar tone of sober explanation. "No, *Signore*. But do you remember how they spoke at dinner, of the new names people are given in America?"

Enzo nodded, and couldn't restrain a sigh. The couple across the table had told of it. Enzo had been readying himself for a land where no one knew him; but he hadn't expected it to be so bad as that.

"Well," Saredda went on, "in my dream you called me by another name. And I don't know how it was, but when you called me that, I felt there could be nothing wrong in whatever you asked of me — even going to America, though I once was certain the gates would stay closed against me."

Enzo smiled, with a lighter heart than might have been expected in one who'd been through so much to find so simple an answer. "And what shall I tell the man your name is, then? Dearest Heart? Queen of the Sea?"

He whispered the words into her ear, and in the same manner she replied with that name evidently powerful to open any door, of iron, flesh, or stone.

"Tell him: Assunta."

The Boarder

In those days, if you had trouble getting by, you took a boarder. Antonia put hers in the parlor with the two youngest children. The older girls shared one of the bedrooms, and Antonia took the other bedroom for herself. It was the only time in her life she had had her own room. Even after her husband's death in Italy, she had had the baby with her.

Who could deny her need of a little peace? She spent her days cooking and cleaning, and trying to earn a few pennies by sewing buttons on shirts (the girls helped her in this), at the same time watching that the younger children didn't fall into the stove in winter, or out of the window in summer. At least her nights she could have to herself. And who knows, some day they might be able to live without a stranger in their midst; soon the girls would be old enough to join their sister Maddalena in the candy factory.

Not that Rosario, the boarder, was any trouble. The poor man had to leave his wife behind in Italy because they wouldn't let his sick child into the country. He sent home all the money he didn't give to Antonia, and every Sunday eleven year old Maria, who went to school, read him the letters a friend had written for his wife. Rosario never complained, though he sighed often. Because of his size, however, you couldn't be sure if that heavy breathing expressed his homesickness or was simply the work necessary to keep his big heart beating under its blankets of flesh.

He was regular in his habits, too, leaving for his job while the rest were still at breakfast, and returning every day at 6:30, as dinner came to the table. So Antonia saw no point in answering the day Maddalena burst in at 5:30 and whispered dramatically, "Is Rosario here?"

Antonia just looked at her. Her hair was covered by a kerchief, like a woman's, and she already had a considerable shape, but her brain didn't hold much more than Angelina's, who was six.

Maddalena stopped whispering; now she screamed. "Ma! You know Giacinta?"

"Why should I?" replied Antonia. "Is she bringing me money?"

"Giacinta DiSimone, the girl who's a dipper and she's only sixteen? They found her with a man, and he turned out to have a wife in Italy, and to save herself she had to marry a man her mother got for her!"

"Why?" asked Angelina.

"Would you like to explain it to her, you shameless girl?" Antonia asked Maddalena.

"But, Ma, don't you see?" Maddalena persisted. "The man that ruined her was a boarder in her mother's house!"

"Is he looking for someone else to pay his rent to, then? Tell him to come to me, he can share Rosario's bed."

"But what are you going to do about me and Rosario?"

"Why? Has he ruined you?" The children looked at Maddalena with interest.

"Of course not," she said, "but who knows what he's planning?"

"The poor man isn't planning anything but to get an extra hour of sleep on his day off."

"I'll have to get married," said Maddalena. "What other choice do I have? Giacinta did, and she's younger."

"And who are you going to marry? Luigi, who hangs around? With what he makes, how would the two of your afford a family? And where would I put you? I don't have a room for you, and his mother won't take you in. When it's the time, I'll find a husband that can take care of you."

"But what are you going to do about Rosario?"

"One thing is sure, I'm not going to throw him out because a girl I never heard of shames herself."

"Didn't she use the pot?" asked Lino, the youngest.

"Are you going to keep on pouring filth into these children's ears," Antonia asked her daughter, "or will you set the table?"

Maddalena did as she was told, but the moment Rosario walked in the door, she nearly jumped out of her skin. Fortunately, Rosario didn't notice: the walk up the stairs to the apartment took the last bit of strength his day of digging the streets had left him, and he always had to sit in a chair looking at the floor for a while before he could even wash for dinner.

But at the table Maddalena continued to behave like a madwoman. Forced to sit next to Rosario, she kept her head facing the opposite direction, as if her neck were paralyzed; she never looked toward her plate as the fork continued working of its own will, so that every mouthful must have been a surprise to her. And when Rosario asked her for the cheese, she was deaf, and Antonia finally had to reach for it herself.

Maddalena jumped up to clear away the dishes when Rosario was only half done. Antonia yelled at her, and Rosario put his hand on the girl's arm. The dish fell to the table with a clatter and a splash, and the children began to shout. At last Rosario took notice.

"Is anything wrong, *Signorina?*" he asked Maddalena, but the girl was now mute as well as deaf.

"You must be tired after a day like this," Antonia said to him. He ordinarily retired as soon as dinner was over, but he didn't take her hint.

"Let me help you wash," he said to Maddalena. Though she cried, "No!", from that moment he didn't cease to torment the poor girl. It was a wonder more dishes weren't broken that night. As Antonia prepared the children for bed, she tried not to pay attention to the sounds in her kitchen, but she unconsciously exclaimed a prayer every time she heard a piece of china dropped back into the basin.

Now Rosario never took his mournful eyes off Maddalena, making atonement for a sin he was unaware of. He did favors for her, like bringing her his dirty underwear for the wash instead of making her come to ask for it, the girl accepting it as gratefully as if it were a nest of poison snakes. He helped her out, not only by handing her dishes to break after dinner, but by reaching the knife to her so that she could slice her fingers instead of the orange. Worst of all, he took to lurking: at the time when Maddalena ordinarily left her bedroom to go to the bathroom down the hall, he readied himself with a towel for her, and leapt out at her when she walked into the kitchen; or if for a moment she forgot about him, he would creep up behind her and suddenly ask if she would like a chocolate. Who but Rosario would have the brains to offer chocolates to a girl who worked in a candy factory? And where did he get chocolates, if not by holding back money that should have gone to his overworked wife and the little girl who, he said, had never been out of bed in her life?

Antonia did what she could to ignore all this, but it wasn't easy. Once, when she had put the children to bed and Rosario had followed immediately, she had been able to sit up with her mending, or to sew some more shirts, and the work itself would become a pleasure to her in the rare quiet of the apartment. But now Maddalena and Rosario were up half the night, it seemed; Maddalena's after-dinner tasks took twice as long now that Rosario was dedicated to helping her. Not one of Maddalena's squeals or Rosario's apologies failed to penetrate Antonia's bedroom door.

The night Maddalena finally succeeded in breaking the big platter, Antonia ran out of her room — she was already in her nightgown — and ordered the girl to bed. Then she turned and said to Rosario, who was crouched puffing on the floor, picking up the pieces, "*Signore*, you are not the servant in this house."

"I'm just picking up the dish that fell," said Rosario.

"And why aren't you in bed at this hour? Don't you work any more?"

"I thought I would help your daughter," he said, but he was shaking his head, conceding in advance any particular argument Antonia would choose to have with him. Then he stood up, arranged the fragments of the platter together on the table, and stared at them, silently urging them to put themselves back together.

"My daughter doesn't need any help. She was once able to break my dishes without your assistance."

"*Signora*," said Rosario, turning his pleading eyes from the splinters to her, "have I offended your daughter?"

"Offended my daughter?" said Antonia, making her own eyes big.

"I'm afraid I must have hurt her feelings without knowing it," said Rosario. "*Signora*, a girl without a father like her — every man should regard her as his own daughter, and should never do anything to hurt her."

"Believe me, I'm no such miracle," Antonia replied. "My daughter does have a father, only he's under the earth, that's all."

"It gives me pain to think that I might have made her unhappy. Don't you have any idea what she thinks I've done? It isn't that I make too much work for her by living here? You don't think I should move?"

"Move!" Antonia cried. "Are you as crazy as her?"

Rosario sucked in a breath. "Is she crazy, then?"

"All right, I'll tell you," said Antonia, "and you judge for yourself. She thinks you want to ruin her, that's what my daughter thinks of you."

Rosario blushed all over his body. "Really?" he asked.

"Yes, that's all it is. Now, are you going to continue breaking my dishes because she has this stupid idea?"

Rosario didn't reply at once. Finally he said, "Perhaps I should move, if that's what she thinks."

"Why? Are you going to ruin her after all?"

"*Signora!*" Rosario cried, blushing again.

"When you ruin her, you can move, not before. Now go to bed."

The next night, Rosario did not help Maddalena serve out the dinner or wash the dishes; what was more surprising, he didn't show up for dinner at all. Maddalena looked uneasy throughout the meal, as if this might be part of a scheme, and he were waiting under the table to pounce on her.

Antonia had a different uneasiness, and after dinner she went into the parlor to test her suspicion. But his trunk was there, inside it his clothes and the letters and photos from his wife. Still, that night Antonia couldn't get to sleep, waiting for the sound of the apartment door opening; might he not be crazy enough to leave all his belongings behind him?

But he was not yet that crazy; long after dark, Antonia heard the door, and his heavy footstep on the kitchen floor. The next morning she caught sight of him when she got up to make breakfast. He was wolfing down a piece of bread, his eye on Maddalena's bedroom door. He was ready to rush out of the apartment if he saw it open.

"Rosario, where were you last night?" Antonia asked.

"We had to work late," he said.

"In the dark?"

"It wasn't dark where we were," he said.

He was reaching for the knife to cut another slice — all the while glancing furtively at the girl's door — when Antonia asked, "And did you eat?"

His hand paused, hung in the air, then returned to his side. "Oh, yes," he said. "I ate with a friend." Then he cast a look at the loaf of bread that would have brought tears to your eyes, stood up, nodded goodbye, and left for work.

He never again ate dinner with them, and Antonia saw him only fleetingly in the mornings, and through increasingly bleary eyes. For every night she lay awake to listen for his return, convinced that he and his weekly payments were about to disappear. After all, how long could he bear it? If her eyes were blurred with exhaustion, his were blind. He was embarrassed to eat much breakfast in front of her lest it belie his story of late hours and a generous friend. One morning she told him that she wasn't going to be able to reduce his board, if that was what he was waiting for, so he might as well join them for dinner.

"A man of your size can't miss his meals," she said.

"I eat, *Signora*," he said, hurrying out the door.

So she began leaving food out for him, as if he were the family pet: cheese, sausage, cold potatoes. Some days he was too proud to eat any, and when Antonia was up in time to see him, the two of them would say a pleasant hello and goodbye while the gazes of both were locked on the dish she had left, with drops of fat congealed on it. But even worse, as far as Antonia was concerned, were the mornings she got up to find the plate empty, and Rosario already gone, so ashamed had he been to confess his frailty.

She fed him enough to sustain him, but without sleep his days — if not her own as well — were numbered. And she thought the last day had been reached the morning Maddalena, who had gone into the parlor to make the children's beds before leaving for work, let out a scream. Antonia rushed in, but Rosario wasn't dead.

He was sitting up in bed in his undershirt. His shoulders were the color of flour, and they had the shape of risen dough. "My God, I'm late for work!" he cried.

But Maddalena was louder. "Stay away from me!" she told him, her body frozen. When she saw her mother, she threw herself on her bosom. "He was waiting for me!" she wailed.

"Waiting for you!" cried Antonia. "This man was asleep! What can he do to you in his sleep?"

"Don't they find ways?" asked Maddalena. "Giacinta was asleep through the whole thing!"

By now Rosario was awake enough to confess. "She's right, *Signora*, I'll leave."

"What do you mean, she's right?" asked Antonia. "What were you going to do, tell me."

Rosario shrugged, and shook his head sadly at the thought of the crimes of which man is capable. "Who knows what was in my mind, *Signora*?"

"Excuse me, two lunatics at once are more than I can care for. It's time for both of you to go to work."

"*Signora*," Rosario called to her as she walked back to the kitchen. "I can't stay! It isn't proper, a man sleeping in the room where your daughter can find him. I'll find another place."

"He's right, Ma," Maddalena cried, "Luigi says he has to go, or I'm not safe."

"Luigi! And what is Luigi to me?" Antonia asked.

"Luigi says any girl but me would be disgraced to live unmarried in the next room from a man."

"I'll go, you don't have to tell me, *Signora*," said Rosario.

"All right!" Antonia said, throwing up her hands. "You can have my room, is that what you want? I'll sleep with the children, you can stay in here, and my daughter won't have to see the hairs on your chest."

"Ma!" said Maddalena.

"What sleep do I get these days anyway?" Antonia asked the ceiling.

Don't think that Rosario accepted her offer without more argument; no, Antonia had to lie and plead and appeal to the patron saint of Rosario's town to get him to agree to a more luxurious life than any other boarder in the city enjoyed, with his own room, and meals served at his own hours. The discussion was very informative for her children, too, who spent the next few days arguing over who slept where, and what was proper.

Lino and Angelina were satisfied to have their mother in the parlor with them, because now they could badger her every night to let them climb into her bed. She forbade it, but once she finally did get to sleep each night — after Rosario had creaked through the front door, and eaten the food she had left for him with much clinking of the fork against the plate, and at last lumbered to his private room as mournfully as if it were the tomb — she would shortly be awakened by the sensation of one of the children's hot bodies stretched next to hers. It was July, and that meant that the windows were open, too. Antonia's former bedroom faced an alley, where the worst noise was an occasional cat on the fire escape, which someone from another window would usually shoo away. The parlor faced the street, where noisy activity never stopped. After Antonia had put Lino or Angelina back in bed with the other, she would lie awake listening to stupid men having stupider arguments, or the clattering of cart horses who wanted, like her, to be asleep, but were being driven through the streets on the errands of their human masters. And in the mornings when she woke (if you could call it that) to find the weekly payments left on her table by the invisible Rosario, she felt for all her pains like a criminal, receiving stolen goods.

Since she was the one who took the money, and listened for his step, and left out his food, she was almost the only one who remembered that Rosario still lived with them. Lino once asked her if another man would come to live there; and even Maddalena, though she still talked about marriage, seemed to have found some peace, and possibly some sense as well.

This change at last made Antonia consider the idea of a husband for Maddalena. She began trying to expand her circle of friends, looking for mothers with sons a little better off. A couple of women quickly expressed interest, but Antonia kept her distance, rightly suspicious of mothers so eager to dispose of their sons.

Antonia made sure that Maddalena dressed well on Sundays, not only to catch the eye of the men who stood in groups outside church, but to impress the ladies inside, for every Sunday one or two new introductions would be made. The rest of the girls followed suit, of course, down to Angelina. When Maddalena took her fancy handkerchief off in the hot sun, and smoothed it over her shoulders, her four sisters did the same. When Maddalena began putting her hair up with combs, all the sisters wanted them. Antonia let them have one each.

One Sunday, when they were halfway to the church, Angelina began to complain and then to whimper. She had forgotten to put the comb into her fine hair, which had a hard time keeping it in. It was soon enough clear that unless she got what she wanted the child would give them no peace, Maddalena would lose her patience and with it her good looks, and the Sunday would be wasted. If Rosario had been with them, as he always used to be when they went to church, he would have volunteered to run back home at his first glimpse of Angelina's frowning face. But who knew where he spent his Sundays now? A pious man, he must have gone to Mass somewhere, presumably the Irish church, where you had to pay. But where did he go the rest of the day? The Irish couldn't read him the letters in Italian from his wife, that Maria used to interpret for him on Sunday afternoons. Antonia didn't like to think these thoughts, so she just told Maddalena to go get Angelina's comb and hurry back. Meanwhile she scanned the crowd approaching the church.

Naturally, today for the first time she saw her *compare*'s sister-in-law speaking to a mature woman wearing

lace on her head. This must be the wife of the *compare*'s
brother-in-law's boss, who had three sons. "Bless you,
Lisa," said Antonia, and the introduction was made. But
where was Maddalena? At last they had to go inside if they
weren't going to miss the Mass.

Maddalena never came, and the boss's wife went
home with a firm conviction of the freakish unruliness of
Antonia's marriageable daughter. Antonia stormed up the
stairs of her building in her impatience to find the girl's
latest trick.

But Maddalena wasn't in the apartment. Only
Rosario was there, looking as if he'd had a wasting illness
since Antonia had last caught sight of him. But it was all
the effect of the last hour.

"*Signora!*" Rosario cried. "I've done it!" Then he
burst into tears.

Antonia sent the children downstairs with Olimpia,
though she knew they would probably get no further than
the other side of the apartment door.

"Rosario! Calm down!" she said. "What have you
done?"

"I've driven your daughter away from you!" He sat
down hard on a chair, put his elbows on the table, and hid
his face in his hands.

"And how have you done me this favor?"

After a few moments, he was calm enough to tell her
more. "You know I don't go to Mass any more, God forgive me," said Rosario.

"How can I know what you do, when you creep in
and out of my house like a thief?"

"I'm sorry, *Signora*. But I always say a rosary on
Sunday, and some people say that counts as much as a
Mass. This morning, after you left, I went out to the room
down the hall, and then came back inside. I was going to
say my rosary, and then walk in the park as I always do on
Sunday. So I knelt down beside my bed — that's where I
pray — and then the front door opened. I hadn't shut the

door of my room when I returned to your apartment, and I looked up, and saw Maddalena, and she fainted."

"She fainted?" said Antonia.

"I think she fainted, anyway. She closed her eyes and fell against a chair. I thought she might have hurt herself, so I came into the kitchen. When she saw me she began to scream. She said I was a bad character, *Signora*; she pleaded to God to help her."

"And what did you do?"

"I kneeled down, to plead to God to help her, too."

"And did He?"

"I don't know, *Signora*. When she saw me kneel on the floor, she cried for her mother, and ran out the door."

"Did she tell you where she was going?"

"Isn't it enough, *Signora*, that I drove her away from your house? You see now why I can't stay?"

"Rosario, if you leave this house, you might as well take one of my children with you and throw him in the ocean, that's how much chance they have of staying alive without the money we get from you."

Rosario wrung his hands.

"Now, listen to me. Today, stay inside, don't walk yourself to death in this heat. Get some sleep. Eat your dinner at a normal hour. No wonder you've lost your mind! And don't worry about my daughter, she'll be back. Who does she know that could afford to take her in?"

So Rosario did stay inside that day, and even joined them at dinner. He ate looking all around him, like a dog expecting the food to be stolen from him at any moment. Maddalena didn't return and didn't return, and the youngest children used this as their excuse for not wanting to go to bed. Finally even the children fell asleep, but not the mother. This was the first night in many weeks that there were no footsteps across the kitchen floor. Maddalena never came home.

After she got out of bed to make breakfast, Antonia learned that while there had been no steps in the kitchen, there were other steps she should have been listening for. She knocked at Rosario's door to wake him, since she knew he hadn't left for work, and thought he might be oversleeping again in his distress. He didn't answer, and she knocked louder. Since all she needed would be for her boarder to lose his job, she went so far as to open his door and peep in.

He was gone. The bed was made up — had he slept in it at all? Even the trunk was missing; the poor man must have carried it on his back down the fire escape. On the bed he had left enough money to pay for two weeks, which he didn't owe her. As likely as not it was every cent of his extra cash.

When Antonia was a girl in Italy, a neighboring family had awakened one morning to find that one of its daughters had not returned all night. Immediately, everyone in the town knew it, and the family stayed at home for days as if they were in mourning. But when you lived in a building like this, who would know which family was being shamed by a girl spied running away? If school had been in session, who would have asked Maria where her sisters had spent the night? Today when the man at the factory gave Olimpia the shirts to bring home, he probably didn't know her last name, and certainly wouldn't see anything odd in her appearing in public. If he thought about it at all, he would assume it was so she wouldn't starve. And wouldn't he be right?

In Italy, the girl who'd run off had never come back. But Maddalena returned at 5:30. The children took advantage of the occasion to begin a shrieking contest, until Antonia threw them out. Then she returned to Maddalena, hands on her hips.

"What makes you think you can come into my house?"

"Ma, I was with Giacinta's family," said Maddalena.

"Giacinta! Giacinta!" cried Antonia, naming the curse that had been visited on her house.

"When I came to get the comb, he was waiting for me beside his bed! And then he chased after me into the kitchen, and got down on the floor! I'm lucky I escaped! What else could I do but go to Giacinta's? I wasn't going to come back and be in the same apartment with that man."

"And there's no need to worry about that now, is there? You know that you've driven him out. He climbed down the fire escape in the middle of the night, like a cat."

"Thank God!" said Maddalena.

"And why? Because your sisters and your brother will starve to death? Because now I have to break my neck finding another man to fill my empty room, and this time we're not likely to get a man like Rosario, no, this time I'll have to take in some man who probably will ruin you in fact, if he doesn't slit all our throats first!"

"But you don't have to find a man," said Maddalena. "Luigi and I will take his room."

"And who says you can marry Luigi?"

"But I already did, this morning," said Maddalena. Then she explained how you could get married in an office, as long as you lied about your age.

Antonia paid little attention, however; she was too busy beating her forehead.

"Ma! How can you be mad?" Maddalena asked. "I did it for you! Do you think I wanted to get married, at my age? I knew you couldn't afford to get rid of Rosario, but it wouldn't be safe unless I was married like Giacinta. How could I know Rosario was going to leave?"

When you can't eat artichokes, you eat weeds; when you can't eat weeds, you eat bark. "All right," said Antonia, grabbing Maddalena by the shoulder. "I'll give the two of you Rosario's room. But every week, Luigi will have to give me his pay from work, just as you give me yours."

Maddalena protested, but she gave in at last, and Antonia tried to calm herself by thinking about dinner.

The children were not yet clamoring at the door; they must have found something to occupy them in the street. How often did she have the chance like this to cook without having to snatch the food and the knives from their hands? And while the onions fried, it occurred to Antonia that as long as there were bosses foolish enough to hire people like her daughter and her new son-in-law, there might still be some hope that her family would live to see another year, if not a better one.

Then Maddalena, who had been taking her time in setting the table, stopped altogether. "And you made me forget what I was going to tell you," she said in an aggrieved tone.

"What is it now?" asked Antonia.

"Giacinta's quitting her job. Her mother told her to."

"Has the lucky girl found a buried treasure now?" asked Antonia.

"Of course not!" Maddalena explained. "It's because she's going to have a baby."

In the Country

Weeks before the move, Pia Zammataro bragged to her friends that she was returning to the life she was used to, a life like the one in the *paese*.

Her husband Nino let her brag, though what she implied was not exactly true. Pia's mother had worked outside the house, and her father had been a day laborer. It was Nino's mother, Donna Maruzza, who had once been a landowner in the *paese* (in older, more prosperous days, before Nino had been forced to leave for America); she was the one who had sat in front of her door, taking payment in grain from the people who worked her fields. And it was Nino himself who, after these two frugal years in America, had taken the ride in Pennington's canvas-topped Ford, and chosen the piece of property he wanted. He bought one that was cheap now, because it was so far out: a few thousand square feet of scrubby trees. But Pennington had hinted that the trolley might be extended along the dirt road that went by the lot, and Nino understood the hint. It was a risk, but you have to take a risk to make your fortune. Nino protected his risk by building a two-family house; the rent from the upstairs apartment would cover his mortgage payments. So Pia had nothing to do with it at all.

But Nino let her brag. It was a good idea to encourage her pride, since she would be taking on new responsibilities with the house. From the apartment where they had boarded, she had never had to go more than three blocks to find whatever she wanted: market or church or the wise women who could comfort her, though they infuriated Nino, by casting for the evil eye to protect her children. In the country, she would have a garden to take care of, and she would need to learn how to take the trolley into the city for her marketing (there was a trolley stop two miles from the house).

For tenants, they were lucky enough to hear of friends of friends, a newlywed couple who needed a place. When they met, Nino held out his hand to them, but Pia stood behind, and kept her distance. Her gesture must have been what they noticed, because Caterina called them *Signore* and *Signora* from the start, and Gennaro bowed his head whenever you looked him in the eye.

The tenants moved in the same day as Nino and Pia. The first Sunday they spent in the house, Nino wanted to invite Gennaro and Caterina downstairs for dinner, but Pia said it wasn't proper. No landowner had ever spoken except on business to her mother, a working woman. Now that she was a landowner herself, how could it be right to speak to the woman who paid rent to her?

It was just as well they missed the dinner. His plate of pasta had such a sauce on it as Nino had never tasted.

"When did you start making the sauce like this?" he asked.

"Always," said Pia. "But when we lived with Lucia, I could never keep her away from my pot when it was on the stove. Now at last I can cook the right way."

"And in the *paese*, before we left?"

"Your mother never let me cook once, didn't you know that?"

When dinner was over, Nino told her that, no matter what she said, he was going upstairs to say hello.

"Well, don't eat, then," said Pia. "If you do, they'll think we don't know how to act, and are trying to be friends."

"I won't eat," said Nino. "It seems to me I've lost my appetite."

Nino didn't eat with his tenants, and poor Caterina was convinced her food wasn't fine enough. But he did say more than hello. He offered to play seven and a half with Gennaro.

Gennaro was overcome by the honor. At first, in fact, Nino thought that politeness made Gennaro play so badly. But as Gennaro followed each hand by a new excuse, Nino realized that he had taken for a tenant the worst card player he had ever met. Gennaro invariably thought Nino was bluffing when he wasn't, and wasn't when he was. He'd never stop when he had a six showing, but always asked for another card, which broke him. He was always counting on getting the *matto*; even if there was only one in the deck — as Nino reminded him — you had to get it eventually, didn't you?

"Next time," said Nino as he left, "let's play for matches."

The first Saturday, when he got home from work early in the afternoon, Nino brought Pia and her children into town for the marketing. He showed her where to get off the trolley, and where to change, and how to go from the station to the shops and stands she favored. Then he left her to buy, and went to look for men he knew.

He found several of them standing outside the barber shop, freshly showered and shaved. They said they had missed him, but Nino confessed he hadn't returned the favor; he'd been too busy planning where to put his garden, and what he'd build on the adjacent lot when he bought that, and what to do with the rest of the money he'd make. He promised he'd invite them out when the garden was blooming, so that they could envy him.

Nino felt all the more impatient for his garden once he got home and saw Pia's purchases: an eggplant with so many bruises you thought that was what had turned it black and blue; greens that looked like they'd already been cooked, and cooked too long; six eggs, three of them cracked.

"It was the best they had," Pia said, shrugging, when he asked.

The next Saturday he stayed home while she shopped, to dig the plot. He dug it so large that he had to make a mental list of the people he'd give his extra produce to. Who could blame him for rewarding himself by imagining the looks and words of admiration his vegetables would elicit from those lucky few?

When Pia got home, she was distressed that she couldn't find the ingredients for her Easter baking; it was what she had made the trip for. She accused Cicciu of having eaten them all.

"Would he be running around like this," Nino asked, "if he'd eaten a pound of ricotta?"

"But what else could have happened to it? And the nuts, I'm sure I bought two kinds, a bag of each. I meant to."

"And did Cicciu break the shells with his teeth?" Nino asked. "Maybe you forgot to buy them."

"Or did I leave them on the trolley?" Pia asked herself. "How can I remember what I do, with the child pulling me here and there and the baby breaking my arm?"

"Are these the freshest fruit they had?" Nino asked, holding up a brown orange. But Pia only shrugged. "There must be a drought," said Nino.

The drought was a long one: the next two weeks, Pia came home with the same damaged goods, and usually without what she had intended to buy. In honor of the drought, of which his wife's bruised vegetables were the only visible sign, Nino brought a few extra pails of water to douse the seeds in his garden. When the watering was through, he would play cards with Gennaro, who waited for him on the back steps with the deck in his hand. Never was man so eager to lose as Gennaro; never a man so surprised at the fact that he couldn't draw by will alone the one card he wanted from the deck.

The third time Pia came home with the same story, Nino said to her, "You had children when we lived in the city, but I don't remember that you ever left your shopping bag in the street, or bought an eggplant we don't need when you went for onions. How did you do it then?"

"My friend Paola looked after the children, or her mother if Paola wasn't home. Lucia always went when I did, and she had a very good memory. I liked to shop with her, except she made me put back the pieces I wanted to buy; she made me take vegetables that were too hard, and fruit that wasn't ripe yet."

"I see," said Nino. "So the drought is over."

"What drought?" Pia asked. Instead of explaining, Nino said that he would do the shopping next Saturday, and she could stay home with the children and weed the garden.

"But don't you play cards on Saturday?" Pia asked.

"If Gennaro comes looking for me, tell him to play with Cicciu."

"But the child isn't three years old!" Pia observed.

"You're right," Nino replied. "Tell Cicciu to let Gennaro win a few of the hands."

When you live in the middle of the forest, many different kinds of weeds find their way into your garden. Was it Pia's fault if the more exotic American weeds looked just like the plants that grew in her mother's garden, or if the tender seedlings of American vegetables looked like Sicilian weeds? Pia didn't think so, and she burst into tears when Nino, home from the market, reprimanded her for her efforts in weeding. The baby, lying on his back on a blanket, joined in the noisemaking, and at the sound Nino looked around: in his family, tears never flowed from only one source at a time, but from three.

"Where's Cicciu?" he asked.

"My God!" cried Pia. "I forgot him! He's run away! He's lost!"

But they found Cicciu in the first place they looked. "Think of it," said Caterina, when she opened the back door to them, "he climbed the stairs all by himself to see me."

"He could have fallen and been killed!" Pia lamented.

"And who would have been to blame?" Nino asked her.

"Ah!" cried Pia. "Why did you make me come to live where there are stairs?"

"We used to live on the fourth floor!" Nino replied. "How did you get there? Did you fly?"

The following Saturday, when Pia was about to leave for the market, Nino told her to ask Caterina to shop with her.

"But why?" asked Pia.

"To make sure you don't leave your head behind you," he replied.

"No, Nino," Pia answered, shaking her head gravely. "If she wants me to shop with her, she should ask me."

When he insisted, she sat down in a way that clearly indicated she would never rise again. "Is this why you took me from my mother?" she asked. "To make me act as no woman in my position has ever acted?"

So Nino went upstairs himself, and asked Caterina if she would accompany his wife for her marketing. She glanced at her husband.

"What's the matter?" Nino asked him.

Gennaro smiled politely and shook his head. "Nothing, nothing. She's a little tired, that's all. But of course she'll go," he went on, stopping Nino, who had tried to interrupt. "You and the *signora* are so good to us. It interests me very much to play cards with you."

"Oh, yes, I'll go," said Caterina eagerly.

"But there's no reason, if you already went," said Nino. "Forget that I asked."

The two women went. Nino watched them walk away, Pia always a step ahead and careful not to look back. It was as if the two of them were strangers on the cobblestones of a city street, and not the only people visible whichever way you looked down the dirt path.

The next time, Caterina left her marketing until the afternoon, and Nino felt less like a tyrant as she followed Pia out of the house. But what tyrant took care of his own children, as Nino did now? They constantly called his attention away from his card game with Gennaro — though it had to be confessed, he would still have won if he had played blindfolded.

When the plants were up and blooming, Nino kept his promise, and invited two of his friends to make the trip out to see him on a Saturday afternoon. They talked of nothing but the difficulties of the voyage, as if coming out from the city were worse than crossing the ocean. They made fun of Nino, trammeled with children, though Nino tried to ignore the small ones as much as possible. Naturally, the baby chose this day to grieve for having been born — or so Nino concluded. What other subject could have occupied the infant's brain for so many hours, constantly refreshing his screeching throat? When they played seven and a half amidst the din, Nino lost even more than Gennaro, and it was pennies, not matches. Gennaro was quite proud of having lost only a day's wages in two hours of play, since Nino did so much worse.

The men from the country would no doubt have lost more to the men of the city had not the game come to an abrupt halt. Caterina burst through the front door, and ran gasping into the kitchen. Pia had fainted on the road. She had woken up, but didn't have the strength to walk home, and Caterina couldn't manage the *signora* and the groceries too. The men went running, and among them carried home the woman, the cheese, and the vegetables.

When Pia was sitting on a chair in the kitchen, Caterina said, "I believe she's expecting. Is that it, *Signora?*"

Pia thought about it and said, "Give me a glass of wine. If it tastes good to me, then I'll know, because my mother always drank it when she was expecting."

At least now the baby was quiet, rocked in Caterina's arms. "Only think of it," said the childless woman, nodding to her burden, "another angel for this family."

"I see that you're right, Nino," said one of the visitors. "In some things, you are getting rich."

So Nino once more did the marketing himself. But at least he ate better food; for he'd told Pia, since she was pregnant, she had to have Caterina help her out around the house. Caterina agreed, although Nino had to force her to accept a cut in the rent as payment for her work. He told her he wouldn't let her do it if she didn't take something. It was only fair.

Caterina was up and down the back stairs all day now, and her eyes were always tired. But at least Nino could keep the food on his stomach, and when he returned home from shopping, neither of his children had disappeared.

Although he was now making so many trips to the city, he had no time to see his friends, for he had to get home to work in the garden before dark. One day he ran into an old acquaintance, who asked why they never saw him any more. Nino replied that this was the price you had to pay to get rich.

"Rich?" the friend said. "So have they started building your trolley?"

It would be any day now, Nino assured him. But the friend claimed that there wasn't a man working on the crews he didn't know, and not one was digging in Nino's direction.

"That's because the line by my house will be the best one. They don't want it made by Italians," Nino explained.

When he walked home from the trolley stop that day, it occurred to Nino that if he had picked up one stone and put it in his pocket each time he made that journey — to and from work on weekdays, the market on Saturdays, church on Sundays (Pia went, while he waited outside) — he'd by now have dug a path wide enough for three trolleys, if not deep enough for a subway.

As he approached his back door, Caterina saw him from the top of the stairs and came down to speak to him.

"All right, tell me," said Nino, wearily dropping his bag. "Is she dead?"

"Dead?" asked Caterina. "Who?"

"My wife," Nino explained. "Or has she put one of the children into the stove?"

"Why do you think that, *Signore*?" Caterina asked in return.

"What is it, then?"

It was her month's notice, that was all. The work of two households had proven too much for her. And they had found a cheaper place, closer to Gennaro's work. For them, the location had turned out to be a little inconvenient.

"Inconvenient?" Nino repeated. "Inconvenient?"

He reached down, dug his fingers into the soil, and uprooted a clod of earth.

"Do you see this?" he asked.

Caterina nodded.

"This is the center of the world!" And he hurled the clod up into the air, letting the dirt rain down on him. Then he picked up the shopping bag and stomped into the house.

But Pia and the children were taking their naps. Breathing hard, he forced himself to be quiet. He stood clutching the edge of the kitchen table, and listened to Caterina's slow step on the stairs. When he had calmed himself, he put away the groceries. Then he took a spoonful from Caterina's sauce, simmering on the stove. Finally, he went out the back door and up the stairs to his tenant's apartment.

"Gennaro," he said when they let him in, "why do you want to make me a poor man?"

Caterina was still cowed, but Gennaro smiled charitably. "I know you'll understand, *Signore*," he said. "We have to watch the pennies, now that my wife is like yours."

"Like mine?" said Nino. "What woman is like my wife?"

"She spits," Gennaro explained modestly; for that's how *paesani* say the woman is pregnant.

"I see," said Nino.

"Caterina and I don't have a future like yours to look to. We have to save."

"Yes, I have an excellent future," said Nino. "When you move, and this apartment sits empty for months, then how rich I'll be!"

"But when the trolley comes," said Gennaro, "then everyone will move here, and your land will be even more valuable."

"Which is going to come first, do you think, the trolley, or Christ?"

"Let's play a game of cards, *Signore*," said Gennaro. "It makes you feel better."

So Nino played one more game. When all the matches had made their inevitable way to his side of the table, he looked down at them and said, "Perhaps the cards are telling me to burn the house down."

"I'm sure you'll find other tenants soon, *Signore*," said Caterina. "You found my husband, didn't you?"

"How would it burn?" Gennaro said. "Your house is made of stone."

When Nino got back downstairs, Pia was awake. As he changed his clothes for working in the garden, she inspected his purchases.

"Why do you buy sausage?" she asked. "Just buy the meat, and I'll make it the way my mother taught me."

"Soon there won't be money to buy anything at all," Nino replied. "Gennaro and Caterina are going to move out."

"They are? Who's moving in?" Pia inquired.

Considerate of her condition, Nino didn't answer with the first words that came to his mind. Instead, he said, "I hope it's someone who can play cards, someone with a brain in his head."

"I'm sure it will be," said Pia. "All my life, wherever I go, the people with brains, they stick to me."

California

Every now and then Lino's friends used to talk about their fathers. Frankie's Pa had it in with the cops, so he could work any corner he felt like. To hear him, you'd think shining shoes was just a little below running hooch in profits. Mickey's father had gotten him moved inside for the winter at Gianelli's, and back out again in the summer, since Gianelli owed him one from the old country. Even Angie, whose father hadn't worked since the War, would chime in whenever his Pop gave him change for the nickel dump.

Lino himself had been only a baby when his father had died; that was back in the *paese*, before Ma had decided to move them all to America. So he had never had anybody to treat him to free tickets to the movies, or to get him a better job than choking his lungs sweeping up at the workshop of one of his mother's *paesani*. All the same, Lino had an answer ready to his friends' bragging. If his father had been the one to bring the family over, wouldn't he have been smarter than to get off at the first stop?

"Cripes!" Lino would say to his friends some winter days, as they leaned against the wall of a subway station trying to keep warm. "Your fathers grew up in the tropics, you'd think they'd have the sense to move somewhere besides the North Pole!"

And it wasn't only the weather. Hadn't his friends agreed that, if you had to work, California was the only place to do it? Most of the jobs there were sitting down —

driving limousines, or getting your picture taken — and even at that, with fruit dropping out of the trees, how many weeks a year would you have to listen to a boss yelling at you? Lino knew enough of his father to be sure he would have taken the family straight to California, if he'd been the one to bring them to America. He was a peddler, Ma had said, and Lino considered that proof enough of brains in a country where there were maybe three people who could count.

Not that Lino blamed his mother for dumping him and his sisters here. Who could be surprised that she'd be afraid to go anywhere except the one block in America where the people she knew had gone before her? She was only a woman, after all, and not an especially sharp one. Look at how she handled her money, for instance. She had been earning extra for a year now. (She'd spent the first fourteen years taking care of her young ones, while the older children supported them; then she'd had to start all over with his sister Madge's regularly produced kids, until Sara, Madge's first, was old enough to watch the rest.) But after that year, what had she saved? Not a dime: Lino knew it, because whenever he asked her for carfare to Castle Island or money for the swan boats, she always turned him down. Small wonder, when every minute she was buying another pair of shoes for one of Madge's kids.

On top of that, once Ma started working, Madge charged her rent. Pa would have put his foot down, if he'd been alive, since it wasn't Madge's apartment, after all. It was the first place Ma had been able to afford after they stopped boarding. But when Madge got married, instead of finding her own place she moved her husband right into Ma's. From that time, since she and her husband were making most of the money, Madge acted like she was the queen. And what did Ma do but put up with it?

This weakness of Ma's, at least, Lino had to admit he shared. After he had started working, Madge had demanded room and board even from him, her own brother;

and he hadn't had the heart to refuse her. With softness like this, he sometimes wondered how he would ever save to get to California — especially when it seemed like every week it was his turn again to treat his friends to drinks and rides at the beach. Yet he had to get there: wasn't it the least he owed his mother? He was naturally going to move her out west, too. American as he was, he still had enough of his father in him to acknowledge the responsibilities of an only son.

In the summer, at least, he could occasionally forget about the better life that awaited him, and Ma too, in California. Those of his friends who had stayed in school after the eighth grade were off for the summer, and what fun could they have without him? And about the middle of July, the water got warm enough to swim in. But one August day, he got his punishment for this short-sightedness — surely no less culpable, in its way, than that of the craven *paesani* who had settled on this cold Atlantic shore.

It was a Saturday, when Compare Joe would give Lino his pay, and free him from his chains at noon. Knowing this, Madge was always waiting at home, with her hand out. But today, when Lino told her he didn't have the money for this week's rent (he had borrowed from Frankie last week, did she expect him to welsh on a debt?), she threw a fit.

"You think you can spend it all on yourself, and live here without paying a penny for what you eat?" It was a shame the way she made herself look when she was angry; especially since she wasn't much to look at in the best of times.

Lino shook his head. "Maddalena," he gently reminded her — talking Italian to her so that he wouldn't have to hear her accent in English, which still sounded as if she was fresh off the boat — "you know I never objected to paying you. Careful, you'll bite your tongue," he advised her, for she was opening and shutting her mouth without saying a word.

"You never objected!" she exploded at last. "No, because you never paid! It's three months, and I haven't seen a penny!"

"I told you," he patiently explained, "whenever I have it, I'll pay you. What more can a man do?"

For her answer, Madge marched into the parlor, where he had to sleep nights with her two youngest, and came back with a handful of clothes.

"Those are my new shoes!" he cried as she hurled his two-tones out into the hall, and his tweed knickerbockers, just as new, right after them.

"What are you doing?" Ma cried at last, jumping up. She'd been there in the corner through the whole thing, peeling potatoes without looking up, but fidgetting so that you knew she was listening. She did just the same when Madge had a fight with her husband; you could always tell she heard, by the extra speed of her hands, but she never stopped. It was as if she was under some curse, or maybe she thought that she only had to peel every potato there was, and peace would reign. If it was that, prospects weren't good, for every day she brought home more: her job was mending torn potato sacks, and she got to keep whatever shrivelled ones she found stuck down at the bottom.

"Can't you fight inside the house?" Ma demanded. Sure enough, in another second you could hear the unmistakable sound of nosy Mrs. Lombardi's door opening, down the hall.

"Who's fighting?" asked Madge. "I'm throwing him out!"

"And *you'd* be sorry if I left," Lino reminded her with a nod. "By the way, if any of that stuff needs to be dry-cleaned, don't think I'm not sending the bill to you."

But Madge kept it up until Ma suddenly dropped to her knees. At first Lino thought it was her heart, or maybe she was praying. But then she reached under her cot, which was set up beside the stove, and took out the box where she kept her passport and the prayer cards with her friends' death dates on the back. That made him think again that she had some religious reason. But then she fiddled around, lifted something up, a sound of muffled clinking rose into the air, and she pulled out a dollar!

"Take it," she said, proffering it to Madge. That was what Madge had asked him to give her every week — and this was when Lino was lucky to get three dollars out of Compare Joe on a Saturday.

Madge's jaw fell. "Where did you get this?" she demanded.

Lino was just as amazed. "Ma!" he exclaimed in bewilderment. "You mean to say, you've got a buried treasure, and you wouldn't give me a nickel when I asked for it?"

Ma looked at him, twisting her mouth a little as she did so. She only came up to his top button.

"I should give it to you, so that you could go to dirty your clothes in the ocean?" Ma asked. "No: if I've saved, from the money I earned, and by denying no one but myself, it's only so that I can buy a plot to be buried in."

Madge could think only of herself. "And after all I've done for you!" she cried. "To keep a secret like this from the one who has taken you in!"

"And haven't I paid for the clothes on your children's backs?" Ma demanded. "Haven't I worked for you all your life? Must I, then, who have already moved away once from everything I knew, be buried with nameless strangers, where no one can find my bones? For I know better than to think that anyone else in this house has saved a penny to keep me out of the paupers' graveyard."

But Madge went on, so bottomless was her greed. Sometimes, when the dinner bowls had been emptied, you felt as if she was eyeing the fleshy part of your arm.

Lino, however, had a different distress. He could think of nothing else all afternoon on the boardwalk; Angie thought he was sick, because he only ate one hot dog. That evening after dinner — Madge had at last quieted down, and taken the dollar — he approached his mother, who was sewing under the gas mantle. "Ma," he said, touching her shoulder. ("See?" he added by way of a lesson, for at his touch she pricked herself with the needle. Hadn't he admonished her about trying to work in such poor light?)

"Ma," he began again, "I hope you're not really saving for your grave? I can understand that you would be wishing for a rest, after the kind of slavery you and I have to do to earn a *dollaro* here. But you shouldn't be thinking of death!"

His mother looked up at him. "Here?" she repeated. "You don't like the work here? You would have me believe, who have seen what men are put to do on both sides of the ocean, that there is a place where work is different?"

Lino shook his head. "Now, Ma," he told her, with a little pinch, "you shouldn't talk about things you don't know, and that a man knows better."

She drew her arm away from him. "Knows better? You mean, the way your father knew how to leave without a penny a wife and six children?"

There was no question now that her state of mind was ailing. It was always a bad sign when Ma spoke of his father. She had brought him up each time some job of Lino's hadn't worked out. Without a moment's rest, she always rushed him to some other relative or family friend who could set him anew to splitting rocks. When Lino would try to point out to her the wisdom of taking a few days or weeks to consider the possibilities before making his choice — lest he fall into the same costly error (for sometimes the bosses wouldn't even pay him for his last week's work) — she would demand in a frenzy, "Do you want to be as poor as your father?"

But Lino persisted. "Believe me, Ma, I know what's troubling you. It's the thought of me having to sweat blood for a man like Compare Joe. You wish you were in your grave so you didn't have to see it, is that it?"

If Lino hadn't been sufficiently alarmed by the news that she was taking money from her family to save for her last rites, there would have been enough to worry him in the sudden congealing of Ma's features. It was as if some mad fear had turned her to stone.

"Do you think to escape from this job, too?" she said in a hot whisper, seizing hold of his arm. "Don't you know it's the last I'll be able to find you, now that the rest of my *paesani* have seen through you? Do you think there's any other reason I would have lowered myself to beg of that pig-headed man?"

"Don't accuse yourself, Ma," Lino consoled her, though her description of Compare Joe was no more than apt. "You didn't know any better."

"Do you want to know what it is that I know?" She clutched his arm tighter still. "I know that if you lose this one, I'll —"

For her own sake, Lino put his hand before her mouth and said, "Quiet, Ma, you're turning red. Don't worry, who can you trust if not me?"

So he went by Joe's on Monday, just to tell him he was through. He had already made plans with Angie for the afternoon. But Joe wouldn't let him leave.

"Don't you know it's driving my mother crazy to see me working like this?" Lino asked him. "Do you want to kill her?"

"Do you ask," Joe replied, "because that's a pleasure you're saving for yourself? There's your broom." He pointed to a corner, and turned his broad back on Lino.

Nor was Joe satisfied by this rudeness: that night, after dinner, he actually appeared at their apartment door. He gave Lino a poison look, but Lino just ignored him. He was glad that Joe should find Ma bending over the wash-tub. The steam made her dress stick to her, and sweat was rolling down the sides of her nose.

But the sight didn't make Joe think again about causing such suffering. He only nodded his head as if it was just what he had expected, and said, "Didn't I say, Antonia, that it would come to this?"

Ma's mouth tightened somewhat. "How much do I owe you now?" she asked curtly. She seemed to think that Lino had broken the water cooler again.

"I'm not coming for my own sake," Joe replied a little more sternly, as if he had expected a heartier welcome. "If I acted for my own sake, would I open my pocket to your son, who does no more than move the dust from here to there, when he's not sitting on my back steps to count the pigeons, so that he can't even hear when one of my men asks for a cup of water?"

It would have been embarrassing for anybody to be beholden to a man as ungrateful as this. Even Ma, woman as she was, had sufficient pride to find silence difficult; you could tell by the way her mouth was working. But she said nothing.

"No," Joe went on, "it's for your sake that I must act, since you have always refused to act for it. For it seems to me I told you you would regret it if you didn't marry my brother, when your husband died."

"Did you?" said Ma — rather oddly, since Joe brought it up every time they met. "I can't imagine why I didn't want to take in another man, who might have been as much of a help to me as my husband was, or as this one has been." She gestured to Lino, and then slapped a sock on the top of the water.

"And why has he turned out like this, except that you've left him fatherless?" Joe asked with a sage nod.

Ma looked like she could answer, but she held herself in, saying only, "All right, what do you want, then?"

Joe shook his head and replied, "I'm only here to say that, since you've left this boy without a man to teach him what is right, you yourself had better accompany him to work tomorrow, to make sure he gets there — and to remind me why I must open my door to him. Otherwise, I might find myself agreeing too easily to his wish to be free of my pay, which he seems to think beneath him."

Ma closed her eyes, then opened them and looked up at Lino. He was about to offer her some consoling words when, anticipating him, she held up her hand for silence. Then — after a swallow — she thanked Joe for his trouble, and even heaved herself up from the floor to walk out into the hall with him. She could be heard addressing him in a voice less sharp than usual.

When she returned, however, closing the door behind her, her remarks to Lino indicated no lightening of mood.

"But Ma, don't you understand?" he tried to explain, when he could get in a word. "It's owing something to an animal like that, it's knowing what I have to go through every day, that's what has put these sad thoughts in your mind. If you let me quit, you'd see how happy you'd feel! And it's not," he added frankly, "as if you'd be broke if I did it."

Her eyes widened at this last sentence. "You'd rob me, is that it?" she demanded, gesturing to the cot that hid her money box. "You'd deny me my grave?"

Lino shook his head sadly and observed, "If only you'd waited to leave Italy until I was old enough to talk, I would have told you then to take us to California."

Sad as he was, he couldn't keep from his lips the smile invariably brought by that name.

But his mother had never smiled at it, nor did it distract her now from her desperate thoughts. "Haven't I already seen orange trees, in my *paese*?" she asked. "And don't I know they grow best from the bones of men who thought they could escape life's hardships?"

Every morning for the rest of the week she brought him to Joe's before going to her own job, though it meant a mile each direction out of her way. She had to put up, too, with Joe's comments, sometimes made by his look alone, on how he'd told her so. If there was anything that could gripe Lino, it was seeing his mother suffer, even if she brought it on herself. How could he save to buy her way out of misery, after all, on wages like Joe's?

Still, Lino did what he could. That was why, when he got home that Saturday, he had to disappoint Madge again. This time, though, the mother seemed more upset than the greedy daughter.

"What?" Ma cried. "I carried you there every day like a child in my arms, and you've thrown it away again on — on hats!" (So she concluded, foolishly enough, pointing at his cap, as if he hadn't bought it over two weeks ago — and as if she expected him to wear his winter cap in the summer.) "Or is it those *bummi* you hang around with that have taken it from you?"

Lino clucked at this injustice. "How could I have had time to spend anything on them," he asked her, "when I just got out of work twenty minutes ago?" It was true, he had come straight home to change before joining Mickey and the girls.

"Then what happened to it?" Ma demanded. At least she had the sense to ignore Madge, who was standing behind her saying, "Don't believe him! He just wants to take it from my children's mouths! He wants to see them starve!"

"I hate to tell you," Lino answered sincerely. "But Joe wouldn't give it to me, don't ask me why."

It took Ma a long time to swallow this, though it was true enough. Wasn't what Joe gave him practically the same as nothing? Besides, to the small degree that Lino had tampered with the truth, it was only to spare her pain: Ma never liked to hear it when he had played the numbers.

Once she was convinced he was broke, however, Ma didn't let him go, though he told her his friends were waiting for him. She dragged him back to Joe's.

"Is this why you made me crawl to your doorstep every morning?" she demanded of Joe. "To rob me of his pay?"

His leather apron pulled over his middle, Joe didn't move a muscle throughout Ma's tirade, which it must have taken him a while to understand. At last — still without a word, and with a face as rigid as if it, too, were bound in leather — he reached for his red-lined paybook, opened it, and showed it to Ma. A moment later, in mute acknowledgment of this error, he put it in front of Lino, to read to his mother.

"This is today," Joe said — his first words — pointing at the latest figure beside Lino's name.

"Yeah, that's the way they write them in the old country," Lino observed, noting the odd curves and lines. "They do it different in America. You could learn if you went to night school."

He hardly got out the last word for gagging, with Joe's hand suddenly squeezing the side of his neck.

"All right, I bought some numbers, Ma," Lino confessed. "But with a crummy job like this, how else can I get enough to take you to California?"

Ma gave the question no thought, so busy was she in humbling herself — it was embarrassing to watch — to Compare Joe. Though she generally scorned the complaints of other ladies, now she brought up Fanny's operation, and the two years Madge's husband was out of work. And then, when Joe talked to her in a way that made Lino want to pop him, she just stood there and took it. Lino himself would have spoken up, of course, if she hadn't hinted otherwise by holding him so hard by the elbow he had a blue spot for days after.

She didn't speak to Lino until they were outside. (The upshot of her self-abasement was that Joe said Lino could stay on, as if this was a favor.) "So it's true, then, you'd have me lie among strangers," she said, her mind evidently still fixed on her final rest.

"Don't worry, Ma, I'll go first," Lino replied, thinking it would be best to pretend she'd been talking of California. "By the time I bring you out, you'll have a lot of friends waiting for you."

That night, Ma tried to talk Madge out of the rent. After a while, Madge seemed to give in.

"See?" Lino asked his mother, who was huffing and puffing. "I told you there was nothing to it."

But what less should he have expected from Madge? After the lights were out, when he had stepped into the hall to see a man about a dog, the door closed behind him as if by magic, and he heard the lock turn, too.

"What are you doing?" he cried. "I'm in my bare feet!"

"Isn't that how they all dress in California?" asked Madge's hateful voice from the other side of the door.

In no time everybody was up, inside the apartment and out of it. The kids were screaming, Ma was pleading with Madge. "I hope you're happy," he called to his sister through the door. "Mrs. Lombardi is getting a nice shot of my underwear. Don't you ever sleep?" he asked the old bat herself, who was peering out in her nightcap.

At last Ma was the one who broke. "You shouldn't have done it," Lino scolded her when the door was opened to him, and he saw her helping herself down to put her money box away.

The next days at work were hard ones. Ma still brought him there, like a prison guard. But when she caught Joe's eye, much though she had humiliated herself before him, he only scowled. Joe was in a foul temper all week, so that Lino started telling the men they ought to think twice, with a boss like him, about consenting to an open shop. Joe usually fired anybody that talked union; but each time Lino brought it up, Joe just said a bad word and walked into the back room.

After a week like this, Lino was looking forward more than ever to his relaxation. They were all going to the beach this weekend, where the Virginia Reel had been opened up for the first time all summer. (It had been closed because a girl had died on it — some said from terror, some said because her hair got caught, and took her head with it.) Lino was going to pay, since he had disappointed them about the Cape.

So how could he feel when Ma showed up, on payday, and asked Joe to give his money to her?

"Ma, Ma," he admonished in sorrow and warning. "What an idea! Don't you know you could both get thrown in jail for that?"

Being a man, whatever else he was, Compare Joe might have been expected to know better. But he turned it over to her, cool as anything, though the words he offered with it were graceless enough.

"I just hope nobody finds out, and turns you in," Lino told his mother more than once on the way home.

Fortunately for her, however, the cops must have decided to look the other way when they learned of it. Lino had no doubt that they had heard, since even Mrs. Lombardi knew. "So he drinks, too?" she asked Ma that night, in understandable confusion; ordinarily it was only if the man was a drunk that a boss would entrust his pay to a woman of the family. And even that was only when the family was on its last legs — not when one of its members was sleeping, every night, on top of Fort Knox.

He could hardly enjoy the Reel for thinking of how his credit looked. Nor did it lift his spirits to observe his mother, back at home, counting over her change and shaking her head, like a miser whose gold could bring no peace. Averse though he was to profiting from others' losses, what choice did he have, then, but to consent when Attilio at work invited him to join their lunchtime poker game the next Monday? Whatever choice Lino made, though, he made with a will; in the end, he anted up every day that week.

He must have inherited some of his persistence from
Ma: for on Saturday, though he might have hoped she had
learned better, she showed up again to collect his pay.
When she arrived, however, she found that Attilio and the
others were on the spot before her, trying to argue Joe out
of Lino's money.

"He said we could get it from you!" Tilly was insist-
ing as Ma walked in the door. "Why else do you think we
let him play — for our health?"

Ma didn't have to listen to much more before she got
the picture. "What?" she cried, pushing herself into the
circle. "Do you mean to say, this isn't a place of work, but
a place of gambling?"

Joe was already a little red; a man, perhaps, might
have noticed it, and addressed him a more circumspectly.
At the sound of Ma's words, he erupted like the volcano
they said you could see glowing, on clear nights, from the
paese.

"And am I to spend my days watching him, too, as if
he were my doing?" Joe shouted, brushing the men off
with one arm and turning to Ma.

"Watching him?" Ma answered. "As if you didn't encourage him, like these other beasts, to throw away the
money that could feed their families! As if you didn't want
to see me starve, because you think that with my dying
breath I'll call out for your brother, or some other man as
worthless!"

Though Joe's response was not in the kind of language ordinarily used before women, and though Lino
himself, in some sense, could have been said to suffer from
it — what else was it but a dismissal, after all, if a man said
he'd see you in hell before you met again inside his shop?
— still, Lino couldn't blame him, after such unconsidered
remarks as Ma's. Besides, he observed to her as they
walked towards home, there was a bright side to it.

"You know what bad thoughts it brought you," he
said, "when I was working for that slavedriver. But now

you can set your mind at ease." Even for himself there
were consolations, though he was as far as ever from being
able to bring his mother to California. How much could
he have hoped to save for that purpose, no matter how
long he worked for Joe? And though fall was approaching,
when the frost made him think most longingly of that
paradise on earth, Lino reminded himself that Mickey had
just been laid off, and now Lino could spare the time to
keep his poor friend's spirits up. It would have been easier
with a little cash, but just now Ma didn't look like she was
in the right frame of mind to be asked for a loan.

While it was still warm, though, there were things
you could do for free. Lino had plans to do most of them,
that Monday, when Ma surprised him by waking him up
early and telling him to come with her. She wouldn't say
where, and Lino breathed a little easier when she didn't
turn down Thacher, the way to Compare Joe's.

In another moment, however, he realized he had
breathed too soon. Halfway up the stairway of a building
in the warehouse district, he was suddenly overcome by
the smell of old potatoes. "Ma!" he said, stopping. "It's
women's work!"

"Truly?" she replied, looking at him. "Then perhaps
you can do half as much as I." And she yanked him up
after her.

It was no wonder she could think of nothing but
graves: in that room, you thought you were in one. The
only smells were earth and rot. The dirty windows were
further darkened by cages. In the middle of the big table,
around which the old ladies sat — they were all old ladies
— was a mound of crumpled canvas sacks, like a freshly
opened grave.

"*Mio figlio*," said Ma, gesturing with a shoulder, and
they all looked at him suspiciously. The boss, a shady-look-
ing type, didn't like it either; but Ma told him, with one
half-English word to every five Italian ones, that Lino
knew how to sew. It was true, when he was a kid she had

put him to sewing buttons at home, along with those of his sisters who were too young to go out to work. So Lino was trapped.

At Joe's, the men told stories, or complained about their aches. Here, everybody was so silent at first (though they kept looking him up and down, as if he had measles), that Lino thought this was the way ladies worked. Eventually, someone broke the ice, asking her neighbor at the table about her daughter.

"She's growing big," the lady answered with a nod.

"And only the fifth month!" said the first one.

"What do you mean?" put in a jovial lady with some spaces where teeth should have been. "By the fifth month, I was always out to here!" And she was putting out her hand to illustrate her point when suddenly, catching sight of Lino, she stopped, and her smile faded. They all clammed up again, and Ma had to sit still under a new barrage of grim looks.

After a while, as if she had decided to accept responsibility, Ma spoke up, inquiring about everyone's health. One of the ladies took up the gambit, and was having a good time relating her ailments until she came to one she paused before identifying as "you know."

"Yes?" Ma asked encouragingly.

"Well, it's —" but the lady stopped, and gave an embarrassed look at Lino.

"Later, dear," observed a dried fig of a woman, "you can tell *me*." And she gave Ma a look.

The whole morning went like that, with sentences swallowed before they were half-spoken. None of their favorite subjects, it seemed — whether diseases of themselves or their daughters, gossip of the neighborhood, or the insufficiencies of their husbands or their daughters' husbands — was suitable for company mixed as to sex or age.

At lunch, so dense was the atmosphere with potatoes, Lino almost expected the women to reach into the little piles that sat before them and take a bite. Instead, each took something else out of her bag: an orange, a tomato, a piece of bread. Ma had some crackers; she gave him one.

The food seemed to loosen their lips, and the lady who used to get out to here — if you asked Lino, she had stuck there, too — said, "Really, Antonia, is he going to stay?"

"And why," said the dried fig, "should she think of us more than before? Hasn't she always acted as if she was better than us?"

Ma didn't look at the second lady, but said to the first, "If he doesn't, my children won't pay to bury me in holy ground, but I must go to the fields like the sinners in the *paese*."

More than one of them looked puzzled at this explanation; but it was all Ma would say.

Someone must have talked to the boss, though. As they were leaving, he came out of his office and asked Ma if she was bringing Lino back tomorrow.

"The money go," said Ma, opening her hands as if setting free a bird, "my children die." Then, without giving the boss a chance to reply, she pushed Lino out the door ahead of her.

Money! It was ridiculous to call it that, their first week's pay. All that Lino had earned would barely satisfy Madge, even when he reminded her of the potatoes he'd brought home. He wasn't left with change for so much as a shave, and could hardly look his friends in the eye as he cadged for cigars and cream soda.

The next Tuesday, when Ma left the workroom to do her business — it was about time, she'd been holding it for a week — Lino appealed in a low voice to the fat lady sitting beside him.

"*Signora*, if you have fifty dollars, I can turn it into five hundred," he advised her. "It would be good for you, and my mother would get to go to California."

But the lady only looked at him with a kind of horror, and said she thanked God she had no son like him.

The rest of the ladies were just as unadventurous when Lino made them the same offer, during the course of the week — nabbing them as they went to leave, or sidling up to them on the stairs, and speaking quickly enough to escape his mother's notice. They were all old-timers, and women besides. By the end of the week, they drew back when he passed by them, as if he could throw the evil eye.

The next payday, the boss dropped the bomb: he wouldn't need either of them any more, he said. Business was slow, and Lino and his mother were the last hired.

"That year," said Ma, pointing over her shoulder to indicate the past, "these see." She pointed to her eyes. "Now, for you, I'm blind."

The boss just shook his head.

"Fire Carmela," Ma said. "All day she sleep."

"And if your son slept, he'd be doing me a favor," said the boss. "The ladies don't like him; I lose my ladies, and I lose my business. This is one charity" — he looked straight at Lino — I don't give to." Then he went into his office and shut the door.

Ma knocked on it, and kept up her arguments. But after all, as Lino reminded her, it was the man's business, he knew best.

"Besides," he said once they were outside, "now you won't have to think of your funeral all the time."

She had been putting her hands alternately to her forehead and her mouth, like some beauty treatment. But at this she stopped and looked up at him.

"Because you'll bury me in California?" she said.

"Ma!" he cried with pleasure. It was the first time she'd brought it up on her own, maybe even the first time she'd actually said the word. "California — it's where you'll *live!*"

But she couldn't embrace her happiness all at once. Suddenly shrinking up into herself again, she began to talk a mile a minute. "Where you'll live is in my sight! I'll never let you out of it again! You can say goodbye to those bums you spend time with, you can kiss goodbye that bed you lie on, for I'll work you every minute, if there's a job on earth that will take us, and we'll find it today!"

It was hard to know where to begin in bringing her back to reason, but he started with the last point. "Us? Ma, think! Who's going to take me together with my mother?"

"You're right," she said, "I'll do better if I let you be a surprise to them. I'll find it myself!"

He couldn't dissuade her. In another minute, she had escaped from his grasp and was off trying to find work on a Friday evening, in a city where every boss had a chip on his shoulder against a man starting out. Lino had heard enough of their excuses to know. "Is he out of work again, and he dresses so well?" the bosses used to say to Ma. "Is it true he killed a milkman's horse?" they said, when the truth was the horse had only been lamed, and must have been blind to start with, the way he jumped out into the path of the car Lino had borrowed. "Forgive me, Antonia," Lino's godfather's brother had said, "I have children of my own to eat me alive." And if it was like this for a healthy young man, what could Ma find even for herself in a place where there were ten thousand young girls ready to work for peanuts in the factories where girls were taken on? It had only been one of Ma's friends that had gotten her hired at the potato cemetery.

As he walked home, Lino shook his head at the hopelessness of his mother's mission, at the sorrow that would be on her face when she returned. It would have been easier, of course, if he didn't feel so responsible. But how else could he feel, with the blood of his father flowing through his veins?

"Pa!" he called out, regretting what he must do — for almost in the same moment, he realized what that was, and felt the paternal blood doing battle with the bond he naturally felt to the home he had grown up in. True, the fall chill had already come, and soon time would start to hang heavy on Lino's hands, with Mickey having been re-hired, and Freddy back at school. But these considerations were nothing next to the profounder truth that confronted him now: the only hope of keeping his mother out of an early grave was to make his long-delayed move — to head out for California.

Nobody was home yet. The kids were in the street, Madge's husband was still at work, Madge herself would be in no hurry to get home, since she never lifted a finger about dinner. Lino could pack untroubled by any but inward worryings.

Even when he had finished, and had brought Madge's bag, which he was borrowing, into the kitchen, he was torn apart by the thought of leaving. As if to remind himself of the necessity, he reached under Ma's cot, pulled out her box and opened it to look at what had first taught him his duty.

He was surprised, when he added it up, at the smallness of the amount. So that was the sum of what she had been able to save, with all her secrecy. It was barely enough to create a bulge in your pocket. Still, he supposed, it was enough. In California, all a man needs is a start.

His Right Arm

"**W**hy didn't you come to me from the start, Nino?"
Pietro half-scolded, shaking his hands before him with
womanish dismay.

Those cupped hands, held slightly apart, might have
been supporting some invisible infant. Was that what
Pietro meant by the start? (So Nino asked himself.) Did he
perhaps imagine Nino's life would have been different had
Nino been born into some other place, some other time?
Could there be any question that, from all eternity, this life
had been marked down, as in some book, for shame and
defeat?

After all, if it came to startings, Pietro and Nino had
started the same, born in the same Pianosanto, and just as
poor. If the Zammataros had owned a little land, the Del-
Finos had had a little shop; and in any case, both sons had
been forced to go to America. But in the new country,
Pietro had not known a moment of the ill luck that had
dogged Nino — had found, rather, only more and more
wealth. It was Nino alone who, just within the past year,
had been robbed of his job, his twice-mortgaged house,
even the few dollars he had trusted to the bank. He had
had to sell his watch just to move his furniture off the
street.

In 1930 such fates, perhaps, were not unique. Their
frequency was little consolation to Nino's particular suffering, however. As he looked about him at Pietro's richly
furnished home, it was a further sting to Nino's torment

— if not the deepest of all — that he now made part of a long list of worthless *paesani* to come suing for help from that famously generous man.

"We could still take your family in," Pietro insisted, "or at least one of the children, Nino. More wine?" With his last words, he reached to poise the jug above Nino's glass, sitting still untouched on a table at his side. It was one of those little tables found in rich men's houses, useful only for tripping guests, or discommoding them with unwanted gifts.

As to the wine, Nino answered by silently placing his palm over the glass. To the other offer, he replied that Jimmy Torello, with whom Nino was living until he could afford to put down a month's rent somewhere, had more room than Pietro. Only a man of Nino's self-control could have lied so boldly. The parlor they were sitting in was as big as any two rooms of Jimmy's — and Jimmy had only three altogether. Nevertheless, Nino would have shunned Pietro's even if Jimmy had had no more than a closet. Not that Jimmy offered better treatment: quite the contrary. But Jimmy's scowl at his boarder's every bite was in fact the only thing that made the Signora Torello's meals palatable to Nino. That proud man could not have kept anything down with Pietro filling his glass every minute.

It was only for a job that he had come to Pietro, Nino finally confessed. And he never would have come pleading even for that if he had had any other choice. No money was coming in except what the oldest girl, Maria, earned at the box factory, and the few pennies her mother and sisters earned sewing on buttons at home. And the little this amounted to went straight, the moment it appeared, to Torello. There was no other boss left to appeal to, and such bossless work as shining shoes was beyond Nino, who couldn't afford the tools.

"Yes, certainly," Pietro eagerly consented, almost before the visitor had finished making his request. "I can easily find something for you to do. But is there nothing more I can do for you?"

"Besides letting me sweep the floors?" Nino asked. Even from men like Pietro, beggars could expect no better than that. "It's already too much kindness for one day."

But Nino had underestimated his benefactor. Pietro entrusted him with more than sweeping, allowing him the care of all varieties of refuse in the meatpacking house Pietro had inherited from his wife's father. The work left Nino, at day's end, with reeking clothes and bloodied hands, so that this hard-lined man looked all the more like an implacable savage. And when he came home with his first week's wages — came home to the daily sight of his wife and daughters bending over the limp pile of shirts as if they too had been reduced to savagery, leaving nothing of their cannibal feast except the peels — Nino was confronted as well by the sight of Jimmy Torello's outstretched hand.

"I'll pay you board, of course," Nino remarked; but there was already some suspicion in his voice. That open palm looked as if it would take the whole world upon itself.

Jimmy slowly shook his head, and tapped a finger on his palm.

"Are you crazy?" Nino cried, drawing back. "Am I a woman?" Nino's wife and daughters themselves looked up with surprise from their work. Their money was naturally turned over to Jimmy, as such funds would have been relinquished to Nino in his own house. It was for the head of the household to decide how the women's money would be spent, doling out what he deemed necessary. But who had ever heard of a man being denied the money he had earned?

"I keep my money," said Nino, "and I'll pay you board."

"Will you?" Jimmy inquired. "Perhaps your friend Pietro would agree to that. As for me, I'm not so rich."

"And what am I supposed to do?" Nino threw out his arms. "Keep my family living here like pigs for the rest of my life?"

"Do you fear you won't be able to buy another house in the country for this royalty, then?" Jimmy asked in return, gesturing to them. Their top buttons were undone because of the heat, and sweat plastered the stray hairs to their foreheads. "How can you say that, with your right arm?"

Jimmy evidently hadn't forgotten Nino's words, years ago, in bragging about the purchase of his house.

"How will I pay for it?" Nino had asked, repeating his friends' skeptical question. He had been one of the first of his *paesani* to risk such an investment; even Pietro had stayed in the tenements some years longer. "Don't you see this?"

And he had bared his right arm, as if it bore some brand of good fortune. Yet it was blank, as ordinary as any man's. It was sturdy enough, of course, so that he might have meant to put forth no more than the common boast of the working man: that the strength of his limbs would suffice to wring from life the promise that his children would not have to wage the same battle. But Nino had never been known to rejoice in a gift common to others. His very words, though sounding unmistakably with the gutturals of his *paesani*, had meanings of their own, as if a man should say a chair for a table, red for blue, wife for whore or enemy for friend. So now, his compatriots guessed it: he didn't mean his muscle and bone at all. He mentioned the compact strength he shared with his fellows only to mock it. His right arm in itself was nothing, it mattered only in being connected to him, to that Nino Zammataro who was never to be confused with any other man — even those brothers of his blood he himself would have admitted to resembling. What set him apart was beyond mere bodily perception.

That he was set apart, Nino perhaps demonstrated by failing to despair even now. At the end of the next work day he approached Pietro, whose white shirt was clean as when he had walked in that morning. He smiled at Nino as if he were equally pure; or was it that the odor of a thousand infernal barnyards, which Nino now carried indelibly with him, was a pleasure to the older man?

"My daughter Maria," Nino said, "could come to your house."

Possibly this was not the form a request ought to take; but Pietro did not seem to notice. He scarcely concerned himself with the reasonings Nino proceeded to offer, merely nodding to them all, and only once gave any evidence of having paid attention. When Nino explained that Maria was making the best income, small as it was, of all the children, and might therefore save the most after her board was paid, Pietro raised his hand and said, "Board! I won't hear of it. She'll save every penny." It required more effort for Nino to keep from crying out against this offer than it had taken him to keep silent when, in the army, two of his teeth were pulled.

Still, Pietro had one reservation, which he offered with the embarrassment of a house dog who has transgressed against the chief rule by which such creatures are suffered. "Since we're speaking of young people together in one house, Nino, I should tell you that I've been in touch with Rocco Tagliani back in the *paese*, who helped me with my fare all those years ago — you remember him, Nino?"

"And is he in prison now, for what he stole when he was *sindaco*?" Nino inquired.

"Ah, you must be thinking of someone else," Pietro innocently replied. "But he has a daughter the age of my oldest son, Joe — she's a real scholar, has learned everything from the nuns, and finishes her school this year. And Rocco and I thought — for how many books can she find in a poor place like that? — how happy it would be if she came here, if she and Joe —" Pietro finished the sentence with a smile and a little shrug.

Nino had no trouble understanding. "I'm sure she'll have learned much in the convent," he observed, "that will be useful to her when she comes to live with your son. As to my daughter," he concluded, "she lacks the wit, if she had the courage, to chase after a man."

Surely this description was amply confirmed by the girl's response to her father's news. "Must I?" she asked in her fear of strangers — the same question she had asked upon learning, some months before, that she must take the trolley to her new job. "Walk, certainly," her father had answered then, "only you'll have to start back every night the moment you get home, if you're to be there on time in the morning." She had asked the question again when she learned they were to leave the home she was familiar with, and move in with the Torellos. On that occasion, however, Nino hadn't trusted himself to answer.

Reluctant though she might be, she was soon installed at her new residence, and Pietro learned quickly enough how little his family could have to fear from so spiritless a creature. He was soon praising her to Nino, in terms sure to delight the father. So modest the girl was, Pietro marvelled, so ready and eager to help. "I tell her to rest, to save her arms for the boxes," Pietro laughed at his own cleverness, "but she says she loves the little ones, and never gets a chance to cook at home." What could please Nino more than to hear how his daughter had become an unpaid servant in another man's house, and that man too the last he would have chosen to serve?

For his part, Jimmy acted as if there were something illegal in Nino's having removed the girl's wages from his reach. Yet there was no denying that he took in more from the father than he had ever gotten from the daughter, and he contented himself with complaining no oftener than three or four times in the course of an evening.

Whenever his sense of grievance was especially acute, he relieved it by inquiring, "Is it a match, then, Nino? Is the butcher trying to raise his family by marrying into yours?" Nino might have answered, but his simple wife always went before him.

"But how could it be a match," she would ask Jimmy, "when my poor girl hasn't even a dowry, and they're so well off?" So Nino had to turn his attention to her instead, admonishing her to occupy herself with her needle, and to leave the arts of reasoning to her husband.

However Nino himself would have defined Pietro's purposes, he certainly wouldn't have expected theft to be among them. But so it seemed to be when, on the Saturday afternoon when Maria was to come with her pay, she didn't show up. Nino waited until dinnertime. Then he set out for Pietro's house.

He hadn't been there since the day he had begged his job. Every mahogany surface, every pane of glass before the pictures hung on the walls, every piece of china in the cabinet, meant for display instead of use — for Nino could see, in the dining room, that the table was already set — all glared more brightly than before, so that the father might be blinded by the labor of his child in polishing them. What other's labor could it have been, after all, since Pietro's children lolled about, playing with toys or reading books like Turks in the harem? Nino looked among them for the famous boy, Pietro's cherished heir, but saw no one sufficiently repugnant to match his imaginings.

"She's in the kitchen, Nino, we can't keep her out of it!" Pietro said, taking his visitor's arm and leading him to the back parts of the house.

"Naturally," Nino replied.

Maria was holding a colander at the sink while Pietro's wife poured into it the contents of a pot one might have bathed in. The woman had evidently positioned it so that the steam would strike Maria full in the face. The girl didn't even have the sense to close her eyes, but blinked at the burning moisture.

"Pa!" she cried, still blinking — proving that, by some miracle, she had preserved her sight — "are you staying to eat? I made the sauce!"

"Eating is not for me," replied her father, his stomach turning to a fist at the thought. "Did you get no wages this week?"

"Ah!" the girl cried, and slapped her hand to her cheek. "I forgot. Mrs. DelFino said I could help cook today, and I was so excited —"

"And next week," Nino inquired, "will your agitation be the same?" She was to come to him, he concluded, immediately after her next pay.

"But —" a voice piped up. It was a fat girl, with ringlets; for Pietro's demon offspring had followed him to the kitchen. The child seemed embarrassed to finish her sentence, and only looked up at Maria.

Maria seemed to understand. "Ah, it's true, Pa," she said, smiling at the small glutton, "they were going to go to the beach next Saturday, as soon as I got home to watch the baby."

"But you must think of it no more!" spoke up another voice, little deeper than the child's, though it belonged to a youth already taller than his father. Nino had only to look at the face, where a red scratch indicated a recent effort to shave its three whiskers, to recognize Pietro's spoiled son. Suffused with self-importance, this creature now turned his attention to his sister and scolded, wagging a finger before him, "You must remember, little one: Mary isn't here to do your work." Having spoken, he looked around him, with a satisfaction that would have befitted Solomon.

Pietro was beaming. Catching Nino's eye, he gestured silently to the boy as if to say, Have you ever seen anything like it? Nino would have readily agreed that he had not. But all Pietro said aloud was, "The boy is right, Nino. She is perfectly free."

"Excuse me," Nino replied, "I will come for the money myself. I could not consent that your infant should be left alone, when it might choke."

So began Nino's regular visits, on those Saturday evenings when the midsummer light lingered the better to reveal the circumstances of his daughter's abasement. She wasn't always to be found in the kitchen, for her masters could scarcely be satisfied by that labor alone. Once he nearly tripped over the heavy carpet, rolled up and laid across the entrance to the parlor, doubtless for his pigeon-boned daughter to carry down the front steps and beat where all the neighbors might see her. To make her labor worse, Pietro's daughters were pulling the child's arms and pinching her waist as they dragged her about the parlor floor.

"They're teaching me to dance, Pa," the foolish girl cried out, so that she might be heard above the radio.

Another time, he found her in one of the bedrooms upstairs, where the oldest daughter was pulling out her hair in little pieces. Half of it was already knotted tight to her head, so that the scalp showed through.

"Will you make her bald, then?" Nino inquired.

Maria answered for her busy tormentor. "She's fixing my hair like hers, Pa."

Nino looked at the *parrucchiere*'s cabbage head and back at Maria's. "If it were bald," he said, "at least you'd have a chance for the convent."

Another time the smallest ones were taking turns in riding on her back. "You needn't explain," Nino assured his daughter. "No doubt they're teaching you to be a donkey, a trick every poor man must learn soon or late."

The boy was always hovering near as well, holding out his hand as if it were something Nino might wish to touch, speaking as if he read the words from a book. "It is an honor to have you in our house, sir"; or, "I believe your daughter is on the back porch," uttered with his eyes squinting, as if he were an old woman reading the magic drops of oil on the surface of her water pot.

Pietro always nodded at these words, as if they were made of gold. (For Pietro was always present, too, just as, at home, Nino could never escape from Jimmy. All Nino's most intimate family transactions, these days, were conducted in the midst of crowds.) Once Pietro even went so far as to confide in Nino, after one of his son's weightier courtesies, "Wrong though it is to confess, Nino, I sometimes wish Rocco weren't so set on having my boy, do you know what I mean?"

Nino only replied, "You prefer to give him to the priesthood, then?" and turned to demand of Maria where she had stolen the jewels with which she had plugged the holes in her ears.

"Rita lent them to me," she replied, pointing with a smile to the tallest of the girls.

Since that giantess nodded in confirmation, Nino left the subject by thanking her for her effort to make his daughter resemble a prostitute, which was no doubt her purpose. But the earrings were to come back to mind the next time he saw Maria. Most of the family was out front when he arrived. The men on this block had had nothing better to do with their money than to purchase empty patches of grass between themselves and the road, and even once you'd passed those you weren't yet in the house, but had to traverse a pillared porch. Nino insisted he would find his own way to his daughter, and walked into the house and back to the kitchen. When he opened the kitchen door, he found Maria standing unoccupied in the middle of the floor, presumably deciding whether to go next for the broom or a rag.

What he noticed first, however, was that she was wearing, not the earrings, but another female ornament: a crimson blush. With a father's instinct, he knew at once the guilty thoughts that it must signify — and that must have led her last week, had he only had sense to realize it, to bedizen herself with those jewels.

Nino was about to speak to her on the subject, emphasizing in particular the wisdom of her choice — for he knew to what disastrous object alone a sinister fate would have led his daughter's affections — when he realized that the boy, too, was there. He was close by Nino, in fact, just inside the doorway, and with a blush like Maria's upon his smooth skin. So it was that young man instead who became the beneficiary of Nino's remarks.

"Bravo!" Nino cried. "Do you plan just to ruin her, *Signore*, or to give your father the excuse he wants to drive her out of his house, and save the pennies in food she eats up?"

The boy having no answer, Nino asked his question again, in this and other forms, until the ardor of his queries had brought Pietro inside.

"But what's wrong?" he inquired. And even a besotted father such as Pietro had to admit, once Nino pointed it out to him, that leaving an unmarried boy and girl alone together was not a thing respectable people did.

"Ah," Pietro explained, "it's because we think of her so easily as one of our own!" ("If only she could be," he added with a sort of sad wink to Nino — who simply stared unblinking at the wealthier man.) "But I know it's no excuse, Nino," Pietro added remorsefully, "and it certainly won't happen again."

"Certainly," Nino replied, "why should I expect it, when I have seen the sort of respect with which she is treated in this house?"

Whatever Nino expected, the fact was that, from this time, he never found the two young people alone together again, and Pietro repeatedly assured him that he never would. Maria even complained of it once.

"It's embarrassing, Pa," she said. "When I leave the room, Joe's father has to call out to find where Joe is, and both of them are always apologizing to me."

"Apologizing?" Nino asked the wise girl. "So that's what it's called, in America?"

Then came a Saturday when Nino's temper was a little shorter than ordinary. It was early September, and one of his daughters was clamoring for school, reminding Nino how little he had saved for his house in all this time. The need for such matters as shoes didn't stop while he tried to save, and some of Maria's wages had had to make up, in Jimmy's pocket, for her mother's and sister's failings: one week, two shirts had gone back stained to the jobber, so that the next two weeks the seamstresses had had to work for nothing at all.

Jimmy was at his worst, too, perhaps from a similar concern about outfitting for school the two of his children too young to keep away from it. "That match is a long time in coming, Nino," he observed this Saturday afternoon, "but I'm sure it's as likely as ever. And what a lucky man you'll be then! For I'm sure Pietro will give you a better job, then, such as he gave his brother-in-law, the *pazzo*."

Jimmy's words were imprecise. Everyone agreed that Pietro's wife's brother — whom Nino had seen once or twice in a corner of Pietro's office, straightening piles of paper, or perhaps sorting string — wasn't crazy, only feeble-minded. Nino didn't stay to correct his landlord, however, but only strode out of the apartment with a somewhat quicker breath than usual.

When he got to Pietro's house, his breath was quicker still, for he had walked all the way, and walked hard.

"Today you *must* stay for dinner," Pietro said, taking his arm, "for we have things to talk of."

"I have never found eating and talking at once good for the health," Nino replied, "or even certain kinds of listening."

"Ah," Pietro persisted, opening the swinging door to the kitchen, "but today —"

If Nino's breath had been quick, now it stopped entirely. "Is this," he demanded, "what you would have me listen to?"

Before his eyes was the old sight repeated: the two young people in the kitchen alone, with no work on their hands but the devil's.

"I should have explained earlier," Pietro was saying. "You see, she's taken the veil."

Nino looked at his daughter, who was blushing, but wore a foolish look of contentment as well. "And do they let creatures like that inside the convent?"

"But do you know the girl?" Pietro puzzlingly asked.

After a few more exchanges, the truth became clearer: it was Rocco's daughter, the girl in the *paese*, who had grown so enamored of the place of her schooling that she couldn't bring herself to leave it in this lifetime.

"So why shouldn't these two be a couple?" Pietro asked.

"With your permission, sir," the boy was saying, with a bow and a hand held against his heart, as if he were a courtier and Nino the Emperor of China.

"And next time you must bring your wife, Nino," put in Pietro's own spouse, who had joined the mob, "we can be sisters."

"These children can live upstairs," Pietro added, placing his two hands on Nino's shoulders.

Nino twisted away, as from a shirt of fire. "So she can be your servant for life?" he demanded.

"But what do you mean?" asked Pietro with a smile. "We know how to value her better than that!"

"You'd like your son's father-in-law, then," Nino said, backing further away, "to be the man who cleans the leavings of your animals?"

"We must talk of that, too," Pietro said, nodding. "What's the purpose of a man's luck, if not to share it with others? You remember, *cara*," he asked, with a nod at his wife, "the job I made for your brother?" Then he turned back to Nino. "Why should you stay forever at the job you're doing now?"

"Why indeed?" Nino echoed, reaching blindly for Maria's hand, as a man might grope for his wallet before fleeing a burning house. "Or why should my daughter stay at this one?"

With that, he pulled her out of the kitchen behind him, through gleaming dining room and glittering parlor, and out to the street, where he led her in silence as far as the end of Jimmy's block.

There he let her go to find her own way home. For himself, he walked the streets for a while, as if looking for a job to take the place of the one he had thrown away; certainly he was as likely to find one on a Saturday night as any other time. When he finally chose to return to Jimmy's, there were red eyes enough in the house, but at least he had spared himself most of the weeping.

Nino didn't sit down upon entering, but continued to circle the room, as if by the very momentum of his earlier perambulations. His womenfolk kept their eyes on him in silence. It was Jimmy who spoke first.

"I don't pretend to understand your principles," he frankly confessed, "but one thing I do know: the money you've given up for those principles wasn't yours. It was mine." He tapped his finger against his chest, lest there be any mistake.

Nino paused for a moment, as if this were indeed a thought. Then he put his hands down among the shirts, leaned across the table, and offered Jimmy a nod of elaborate politeness, not unlike that with which the former suitor to his daughter's hand had favored Nino himself.

But Jimmy evidently had more to say. "I know one other thing as well. With your rich friends, you've spoiled me, Nino. It seems to me I've become used, these past two months, to the money you've brought home, though I accepted you for practically nothing when I first took you in off the street. But I fear that may be where I'll have to send you again, if you can't satisfy the new tastes you've taught me, and I can't say who else will take you in for so low a price — unless it's that family you seem to feel your blood is so unsuited to."

These words hardly seemed to trouble Nino. Indeed, once they were spoken, he reared back, his smile becoming a laugh, as if Jimmy had fallen into his trap.

"This is the sum of what you know," asked Nino, "and yet you call yourself a man? Let me help you at least, my friend, by reminding you of another thing you once knew of, but evidently have forgotten."

"And what's that?" Jimmy inquired, with his fool's look of suspicion.

"This right arm!" Nino cried, thrusting it out before him, to shake in Jimmy's face a shirt he had seized, flapping like a banner.

Jimmy stared in silence. Possibly he was only stunned. But this was enough for Nino, who drew himself up and began to circle the room again, like a lion, or a man seeking work.

Certainly his gesture conveyed the former. When one more circuit of the room was through, he nodded sharply, conclusively, in what could only be the token of his triumph. It was even more than a lion's: on his face was the kind of exaltation seen only in pictures of saints in ecstasy, so transported that their very hands know not what they're doing, or else invest their deeds with mystic purposes, not to be deciphered this side the wall of flesh.

So nodding, and with one final flourish of the shirt clutched in his fist, Nino sat down, and took up the needle.

Crossing Over

"So we want you," Madge said in Italian, "to talk to your husband's parents." She smiled and sat back in the kitchen chair. Madge lacked a few teeth, but her skin was unworn as Fanny's beside her.

"What are you saying, Ma?" Sara asked. "That she's after Jimmy Cataldo, that lump?"

Madge waved a hand at the unaccountability of love.

Sara put down the feeding spoon, shifted the baby to her other knee and turned to Fanny. "You want Jimmy, my husband's brother? I thought it was his cousin Dominic I saw you walking with — or was that last week?"

"Dominic, ha!" Fanny made a pout with scarlet lips. "I wouldn't marry him if he paid me!"

The baby squawked for more carrots, but just then Sara was seized by prophetic insight. "He dropped you!"

"Can you believe it," Madge asked in disgust, "he's gone back to his old gella-friend." She said the word in English; in Italian, the idea didn't exist. "And after what he's done to your sister Fanny!"

"He'll be sorry," Fanny murmured, gazing off into the distance with a dreamy smile. "He doesn't know that Jimmy liked me ever since he saw me at your and Carmine's wedding."

Sara looked from one to the other of her visitors. "So if Jimmy wants you so much, why doesn't he talk to his parents himself?"

"You know your husband's family is old-fash'," said Madge, reverting to English. "Don't you remember how the old people had to talk about it first, then we had to have them over, and go over to their house, and do everything so proper?"

"Then why don't you talk to her? You're the mother." Sara rapped out these last words. She had not forgotten her own first meeting with Carmine's parents, when her father had had to apologize for Madge, unable to forego her beano game.

"*Poverino!*" Madge exclaimed. In her vehemence, Sara had thrust the spoon a little too far back in her son's mouth. Madge reached vaguely in the direction of the bawling infant, with a fellow-sufferer's compassion. "Excuse me for trying to do you a favor! I thought your father-in-law would like to see his son settled before he dies; I thought he might be a little grateful to your husband for helping out. But if you don't *want* the old man to leave you the house...." Madge ended with a shrug, as if to say there was no use in talking to the insane.

In fact, Sara could make no answer. Her father-in-law had set Carmine and the other Cataldos against each other as frankly and publicly as if for a Fourth of July race. His two-family house in Medford was the prize. Whichever of his sons or daughters seemed likely to take the best care of their mother — that one, he had declared, was the child he had instructed her to give the house to, after his death. (The only one out of the competition was Jimmy himself; having entertained him all his unwed years, his parents made no secret of their eagerness to see him out of the house.) Carmine was as committed to the contest as any of them; and it would surely give him an edge if he found a wife for his brother Jimmy, a man who could only make a dollar — when he made it — as a janitor.

Living upstairs from her mother-in-law wasn't Sara's idea of heaven. But she wouldn't mind a little more room, a little more heat in winter. Stingy as they were in some things, Carmine's parents were prodigal of coal.

"Only, you've got to hurry," Madge added.

"That's right," Fanny agreed.

Sara looked at the two nodding heads. Then she wiped her son's chin, put him down to crawl, and walked over to the sink with his dish.

"Well?" Madge said.

Sara turned, her hands on her hips. "And what makes you so sure that they'd be willing to take her, or that I'd be happy to go on my knees to them if they're not?"

"Don't you see, idiot?" Madge answered. "She's pregnant!"

Sara's arms fell limp at her sides. She looked up and down at her sister's skinniness, in the winter coat she had unbuttoned only halfway. She met the girl's eyes: Fanny raised her eyebrows, in imitation of her sister's surprise. Then she rolled her lips inward, re-distributing their paint. Even Madge's exasperation had not been for Fanny, but for Sara; not for the daughter who slept on the street, but for the daughter who was surprised to hear about it.

"So Jimmy has the nerve to do this," Sara asked, "but not to tell his parents he wants to marry you?"

"It isn't his," Madge put in impatiently.

Sara came back to the table and sat down again. For a moment, she had strength only to look up at the clock and assure herself that the children would be in school for another hour, Carmine at work for two more. At last she said, "Who is it, then?"

"Dominic, of course." Fanny frowned at her sister's slowness.

Sara reached over and grabbed her. "Then why are you talking to me? Why aren't you talking to your blessed Dominic? Or send —" But who was there in all her crazy family? "Send my husband, then. Carmine will—"

"Don't you dare, Sara!" Fanny pulled her arm away. "It's my business. Besides, Dom would just say it isn't his."

"But you —?"

"Well," Fanny replied to the unasked question, "I can't *prove* it."

Sara looked at Madge. "I wish I could say I'm surprised that you would allow this."

"Ah, it's true," Madge modestly acknowledged. "What can a mother deny her children?"

On Sunday afternoon, the two lovers sat at opposite ends of the senior Cataldos' dining room table, a decanter of wine and two plates of pastries between them. Jimmy breathed through his nose, emitting the sounds of an aquatic mammal, while Fanny squirmed like the uneasy ghost of herself. Her make-up was a shade lighter than usual. ("If you want to ruin it," Sara had advised her, "just wear that lipstick, and that rouge, and that dress.")

Who wouldn't feel uncomfortable, with Teresa Cataldo sitting there so grimly, the vertical lines in her cheeks apparently gouged by knives? An empty chair represented old Gaetano, confined to his bed beyond the open dining room door. From time to time, Teresa would call in to him, repeating the answers to her questions.

The answers were all Sara's. Sitting with her husband on the other side of the table, Sara was the one being grilled. It might still have been the day she had met the Cataldos, when she and Carmine were in the places of her sister and his brother. The table, the lace, the decanter and the plates were the same. So was the atmosphere of the house: passing the front door for the first time, Sara had felt that she was crossing over the border into Italy, where she had never been. It wasn't so much the king and queen's portrait above the mantel, or furnishings reputed to have come from the old country — the chandelier of brass dragons, lashed together by the tails — but the hush,

the womblike warmth, the unidentifiable smell, the darkness of the drawn shades. It was as if someone within lay
sick or dead, long before Gaetano had taken to his bed.

After all, as far as Teresa was concerned, Sara was
fixed in that long-ago day; she had never left her seat at
the end of the Cataldos' table.

"*Che fai?*" the mother-in-law had demanded once,
when Carmine opened their apartment door to her, and
she found Sara sitting on the floor with her two toddlers.
"So you must play games, too, like a child?"

When she'd heard Sara was thinking of going back to
work, before little Tommy came along, Teresa had asked,
"Is it that you want to shame your husband, or do you just
want more money so you can be a bigga-shot?" Like
Madge, Teresa had her English words.

At least there was no reason to fear that Teresa
would be troubled by Fanny's make-up. She hardly looked
at the girl. When she asked Sara what Fanny did for a job,
and how far she went in school, and who her godparents
were, Teresa was only asking one question: "And is she like
you?"

Without a glance at Carmine beside her, Sara knew
he was thinking of the Medford house going up in smoke
(or to his brother Pete, which was the same thing). "That
sister of yours!" he'd say. Heir to his mother's strict mor-
als, Carmine had never looked kindly on Fanny. Sara still
hadn't told him about the baby.

As it turned out, though, Teresa didn't seem to be set
against it.

"Your father wants to hear a little more," she said
when the young couple had been dismissed, and Sara and
Carmine stood with her at Gaetano's bedside. Although
Teresa spoke so confidently of his wishes, Mr. Cataldo
hadn't uttered a word all afternoon. The two times he had
tried, he'd been seized by fits of coughing, and given it up.

"Anything you want to know, Ma, just ask her," Carmine urged, cocking his head toward Sara.

"From someone I trust," Teresa went on, smiling at his innocence, then nodding unseeingly at Sara — as if that daughter-in-law were a spot on the floor, discovered after guests had arrived so that nothing could be done about it, but carefully recorded in memory, for more private annihilation.

"She wants to talk to your priest," Sara told her mother that evening. Living only blocks away, Sara went to the same church as Madge and Fanny; Father Dolfini was as much her priest as theirs. But this was her way of washing her hands of them.

"What does he know?" Fanny asked.

"Not too much, you better hope," said Sara, rising from Madge's kitchen table, her message delivered. But she couldn't help adding, "I suppose you'll have to pay him something."

This fact might have gone without saying. But all who spent more than ten minutes in the company of Madge — a woman still surprised and aggrieved that she was expected to pay for the pleasure of riding the trolley — found themselves offering her such advice.

"And to think," Fanny observed with satisfaction, "Jimmy is Dominic's cousin! Dom'll die when he hears about it!"

Madge shook her head. "I don't want to see that priest, he gives me *agita*."

Sara looked at her. "Ma, didn't you hear what I said? If he's going to do you a favor, he'll want you to pay him something."

"Why me?" Madge blandly replied, cracking the walnuts Sara had brought. "It's your brother-in-law you're trying to marry off. What is it to me if you disappoint your husband's mother?"

There was a silence, in which the only sound was the muffled cracking of the shells: Madge used her bare hands. Then Sara said, "To save a penny, you'd let your daughter be ruined?"

"What a thing to say of your own sister!" said Madge.

Father Dolfini gave his consent, for the equivalent of two days of Carmine's wages. Sara was turning the corner from the rectory, mentally justifying it to her husband, when she spied her sister. Fanny was a slim slip of a thing; but the way she moved, even when standing still, there was no crowd big enough for her to be lost in.

Just now, her wrigglings were aimed at an audience of one. It was a moment before Sara recognized him as Dominic Cataldo. In a moment more, she had crossed Salem Street.

"And what are you talking to him?" she demanded, coming upon Fanny from behind.

Fanny jumped at her touch. But when she saw who it was, she only smiled.

"Don't you have more self-respect?"

"You're making me black and blue." Fanny disengaged herself from Sara's grasp. "Tell him it's true that I'm getting married to his cousin Jimmy."

"That'll be the day!" Dominic said with a snort, so that smoke came out his nose. He was scrawny, with a jacket too thin for the cold. "This is a punk," Carmine would have said at sight of him, as he had said of the hot dog on last night's dinner plate, "This isn't food."

"And how many other children have you made, to starve in this world?" Sara demanded.

"What's the matter," the boy asked, with a laugh, "you don't have enough, you want more?"

"Oh, dry up, Sara," Fanny said.

The boy gave a mock salute and slouched off.

Fanny bit her lower lip, then said gravely, "Sara, we've got to set the date."

Sara looked at the girl's belly, wondering if it was Madge's girdle that enabled her to cinch her dress so tightly. "Listen," she said, "it's taken you years to get your reputation, you think we can get rid of it in one day?"

But Fanny just stuck out her tongue.

And what was the point of talking? The fact was, there was no time to waste. Father Dolfini had said he'd visit the old Cataldos on Thursday night. Sara intended to take the trolley out to Medford on Friday.

Friday morning, before she left, somebody came up from the bakery to tell her there had been a call from Teresa's number. Running down to the street without her coat, Sara was sure it was Carmine. The lathe had finally gotten him. But when her return call was answered by his brother Pete, she knew what alone could have pried him out of his bar, in his eagerness to be first on the scene: Gaetano had coughed out his last.

"But did they set the date?" That was Fanny's first question when Sara told her.

Sara ignored it, instructing her sister to borrow something black, and to try to look sorry.

When the time came, Fanny did a good job of it, as if her predicament had finally dawned on her. It was almost a question whether she or the bereaved Teresa looked more stricken at the wake.

At first, Fanny seemed merely irritable. Forced by propriety to stand next to Jimmy, his hair slicked down in stripes on his ivory scalp, she barely answered the mourners' condolences; to her fiancé's occasional gloomy whisperings, she was a stone. But from the time Dominic Cataldo showed up to pay his respects, Fanny all but stood on her head to draw his attention. When he failed to glance in her direction, Fanny began twisting her handkerchief this way and that, so that it was soon as wrinkled as if she had been crying for hours.

For Teresa's part, a widow's natural woe was augmented by her discomfort with a wake held outside her own house. The children had thought that waking Gaetano at a funeral home would please her. But when Teresa listed her sorrows to each new arrival, she never omitted to say that she hadn't slept a wink the night before, knowing the body was not in her parlor.

Disgraceful America! If all was to be taken from her, why couldn't she, too, be taken to the other side?

Hearing such words, the mourners began to whisper their worry that Teresa would try to jump into the grave tomorrow. Even Carmine looked distressed at the suggestion, though Sara didn't know of any old-timer's wake where people didn't speak with dread of such a possibility. It was true, at most graveside services someone of the first generation usually made at least a half-hearted gesture in that direction. Sometimes the widow or widower succeeded in getting into the hole; others were held back in the nick of time; some only quivered at the edge, as if restrained by invisible cords. Little harm was generally done: Sara had heard of only one ankle broken in the performance of this ritual. Still, horror and dismay were considered as essential to anticipating the deed as to rewarding its enactment.

"At least it isn't raining," Carmine said the day of the funeral, when he joined Sara outside the church. He had been riding in the head limousine with his mother and his brother Pete. Even Teresa, glancing at the sky as Pete helped her down from the running board, nodded in satisfaction that the trays of food being brought out to Medford would not get wet.

Fanny's was the only distress that never wavered. In the funeral car, she had whispered to Sara, "How long do you think they'll want to wait before —?"

Sara had just squeezed the girl's hand, a little surprised at the tenderness that rose in her own heart.

"After all, we're sisters," she reminded herself.

She kept a sisterly eye on Fanny throughout the service; saw the girl tremble, fluttering her handkerchief before her face, when Dominic walked down the aisle past them; even whispered to her, "Don't give him the satisfaction."

At the cemetery, while Carmine and Pete supported their mother — swaying slowly and continually, like a diver on the springboard — Sara herself took hold of Fanny's arm, so shaky the girl seemed. Then the undertaker's man distributed flowers to throw onto the casket as it was lowered into the ground. Releasing Fanny to take her own flower, Sara looked over towards her mother-in-law. A carnation clutched to her chest, Teresa reared back, cried out, "*Mio marito!*" — then stopped herself, her gasp of surprise joining the rest. For Fanny had plunged before her, landing with a hollow thud on the mahogany veneer of Mr. Cataldo's coffin.

Since Fanny rode a different car back from the cemetery, Carmine's sisters felt free to express themselves.

"Poor Ma!" said Mary. "As if she didn't have enough to break her heart, without that crazy girl making a mockery!"

"Who did she think she was kidding, even if she is marrying Jimmy?" Lena demanded. "What did she meet Pa, maybe once, twice?"

Sara would have liked to defend the girl. No one knew better the reason for Fanny's distress, her exposure sure to come before any wedding could decently be scheduled. And no one was more schooled than Sara in distinguishing the false from the true in Fanny's performances. There could be no doubt: if ever her young sister had touched the border of madness, it was at the moment of her premature descent into the grave.

All the same, Sara could not deny what she had seen when Fanny was helped up that wall of frozen dirt. As soon as her head was above ground, Fanny's eyes had darted, incorrigibly, to where Dominic Cataldo stood gaping with the rest. When she had found him at last looking her way, something not unlike a smile had passed over Fanny's face.

Any remaining hardness of Sara's towards her sister was gratified back at the Medford house. Enthroned in the parlor, Teresa didn't lose for a moment her firm hold on Fanny's hand. As long as the old lady had not cast the girl off — and what else did that grasp imply? — Sara was content that Fanny should begin to understand something of the yoke under which she herself had suffered for twelve years of married life.

Nor was this the only power that Teresa exerted. When the most intimate mourners came up to speak to her, she insisted that they include Fanny in their conversations. (So she had demanded that Fanny ride home with her, in the first limousine.) She refused the offer of food at any other hands, requesting an occasional sandwich or slice of cake only from Fanny herself.

Then, as the day grew late, Teresa raised a hand, quieting them all.

She had thought, she said, that the heart was dead; that respect for elders was no more; that affection and piety had been washed away by the tears our mothers had shed in placing on our cheeks the final kiss of parting on the other side of the sea.

("She studied to be a nun," Sara heard someone murmur in explanation of this erudite discourse. "And from what her husband used to say," observed Lena's husband Al, "she never stopped studying.")

The speech went on, becoming more particular in its references until there was no doubt of the incredible fact: it was all in praise of Fanny. Jimmy understood it, for he began to blush even before Teresa's last sentence, whose purpose was to announce that she invited them all to her son's wedding, to take place in no more than a month —

"so that I might still be alive to see it with my own eyes," Teresa concluded.

"If she dies, it won't be from lack of breath," someone muttered. But Fanny was glowing.

With a wife's instinct, Sara knew that Carmine, behind her, was also turning red, though not with contentment. They had been too successful: Fanny had gone all too far in winning Teresa's approval.

"To think of that little — getting my father's house!" So Carmine fumed that night, omitting the word out of charity, or perhaps because, by then, he had used up his vocabulary.

"Well, there's no telling," said Sara, not for the first time, as she buttoned up the baby in one of her husband's cast-off shirts, against the night air.

But after all — so she sought to console herself — how comfortable would they have been in Teresa's house, once that lady found out that her son's name was given to a six-months baby?

The next Sunday, the banns were announced in the Medford church. Fanny was there, at Teresa's command, and seated next to her. Sara was at her other side. Dominic Cataldo sat a few pews away, as it happened; but Fanny carefully avoided his eyes.

Which made it still more of a surprise when Madge dropped by the next day, to report the elopement.

"That's what that old lady gets, for being so high, and making us pay the priest. And is that all the cookie you've got for your children?" Madge added, gesturing to the dish of pizzelle she had just polished off.

"What she gets?" demanded Sara, pushing the dish away. "You mean, that she's missed the chance for a grandchild from the wrong side of the sheets? And tell me, what has my husband done, then, to deserve this?"

"Deserve what? Now he can get the house again, can't he? You told me just yesterday you wouldn't be surprised if the old lady was going to give it to Fanny, instead of Carmine. But now that she's married that Dominic, I don't think your mother-in-law would give it to her — do you?" Madge puckered up for a moment, as if struck by the thought.

"Why not?" cried Sara, throwing her arms wide. "My sister gets everything else she wants, no matter what she has to do for it!"

"The way you talk about that girl," Madge admonished her. "And now, when she's lost the baby!"

"Lost the baby?" Sara paused, her arms suspended in the air. "What are you talking about?"

Madge nodded weightily, partly to acknowledge the tragedy, partly to prolong this moment of superior information. "She must have lost it when she went into the grave."

Sara slowly lowered her arms; opened her mouth, shut it; shook her head once, as someone might do to jar the eyes into focus. "But it's impossible. I didn't hear anything of this — and how could you not have known? You've been with her every day."

"Well, I don't know how it happened," Madge admitted, "but she told me, and do you think she'd lie to her mother?" Besides, why all the questions? You were so concerned with what your husband's family would think, I'd expect you to be happy!

"Isn't it just as if" — Madge waved hopefully at the plate bare of sweets — "isn't it just as if she was never pregnant at all?"

Asphodel

1

As soon as they pulled into traffic, Pia Zammataro began to cross herself.

"*Ma che?*" demanded her husband Nino. He knew what she was doing even when she sat behind him. "You never rode in a car, in America?"

"But look at the houses, Nino!"

She gestured to a gutted building, exposed walls black with char. In the next block, a swag of blanket hung from the landing of an outdoor stairway, a family conducting its chilly days behind. Further on, a pile of stone abutted the only remaining corner of a house, like wax wept by a candle. Debris was everywhere, though for Palermo the war had ended five years ago.

"Even when we were poor, Nino, we never saw anything like this. And now" — Pia stroked the narrow seat beside her, and shook her head — "now, we're rich enough for a taxi."

"Why not just give him the knife to cut our throats with?" her husband cried, waving at the driver. Nino didn't trouble himself to say it in English. But the young man took no offense, still in good humor from a fare that was more than two weeks' pay.

"And would you have liked to spend the night in the gutter," Nino asked his wife, "waiting for tomorrow's bus?"

"Believe me," the cabbie observed, "it might not have come even then. You've got to know how to get the gas, understand? Besides, why should you show up at your *paese* in a bus, when you can arrive like kings?"

Pia let out a gasp, perhaps at the idea of such presumption, perhaps because the cab's rear tire had just rebounded from a pothole. American though she might be, Pia had never grown used to cars. She looked just as uneasy in the new coat buttoned tightly about her roundness. Her veiled hat, for all the pins that anchored it, sat precariously on her steel-gray hair. She reminded the cabbie of his mother-in-law: a country woman, most comfortable walking, and that barefoot.

"I thought I'd heard that kings were gone from this place," said Nino, "and the proud brought low."

The cabbie glanced over at him. The old man was pleased with his own wit. He didn't smile, as a more human creature might have; but there was a certain icy gleam in his eye.

"Not all of them," the driver replied, setting his own lips as tightly.

Such masculine restraint was beyond Pia. "Oh, yes," she said, "the priest came over to America, and told us all about it. The richest man in Pianosanto himself lost everything in the war, and went to jail, too, they say. You can think what a fall it must have been, if it softened my husband's heart, and made him decide to visit, when we haven't returned in forty years. Our *paesani* have come many times, especially since the war, to help the poor starving, but he wouldn't consider it until the *padre* came over and told about Gianni Leoni, and the next thing, my husband says we're going too! You can imagine how I was surprised, since it was Gianni that made my husband poor, years ago —"

"And do you think this man wants to listen to you!" Nino cried, turning so violently in his seat that he bumped the cabbie's shoulder and almost swerved them into a ditch.

"Watch yourself!" the driver cried.

But Nino had no attention to give him. He had been holding himself in through Pia's monologue, his hands balled in fists. Now that he had let go, he must continue, like the kettle even after it's taken off the fire.

"Fool! Hard head! Are you a parrot, that you must talk without sense?"

"But Nino," the wife answered with sincere puzzlement, "you always said that Gianni took your father's money, and your mother's house, and made you go to America. And even when we lost our house there, you said it was Gianni to thank."

After his last words, the old man had shut his mouth tightly, and sat silently working his jaw as Pia went on. Perhaps he was embarrassed to have shown so much before his hireling. When he spoke next, it was with greater dignity.

"If there is that Gianni to thank for anything," he said slowly, looking straight ahead, "it's for chaining me to this one." He gestured with a thumb towards the back seat. "It's why I've returned."

"Ah, certainly," answered the cabbie, practiced in agreeableness with rich Americans. They always had to tell their life stories, and he was not at all sure that Nino's raging was harder to take than the heartiness of the ones who put their hands on his back and asked him if he ate every day whatever trash they remembered their old mothers feeding them on. Sardines, they said, surely you'll go home tonight to *pasta con sarde.* Of course, he'd answer them, though one bite of any fish made his throat close up and his skin turn to nettles.

"Yes," Pia said, with a complaisance more remarkable than the driver's, "it's right that we give our thanks, especially to a man who's grown so poor, now that we're rich again. Though I hated to leave the children, for who knows what will happen, at our age? But I've never even seen the mother's grave." She spoke of this sight wistfully, as if it were a luxury beyond her deserving.

Pia found more to say as they drove on, keeping up a constant chatter against her evident terror of the ride. At every curve or sudden stop, she clutched the seatback behind the driver's head, until his shoulders grew stiff anticipating the jolts. She spoke of her town's *festa*, which they would be staying to see (though, of course, it was celebrated in America too); of the color of the sky, surely foreboding rain; of the money Truman would continue to send her husband — even, as her children had assured her, while he was in a different country; of the remembered taste of prickly pears, brought to mind by the passing cacti, the only green in the rocky landscape. Now and then her voice dropped below audibility, except to her husband, always ready to take up a false word or disputable fact. Occasionally she grew silent — not responding to his arguments, but shocked by his blasphemy into voiceless prayer. His cries and mutterings hardly indicated any more considered attention to her. The two of them were like sleepers, rolling over unconsciously at an elbowing just as unconscious, but never waking from their separate dreams.

At last a sign showed Pianosanto, across a valley where green blades of wheat thrust through the soil. Climbing the slope, they passed almond trees in bloom, and a scrub of wild wheat and asphodel. Pianosanto was just one more hill town, its roads unpaved, its crumbling houses leaning into or away from each other as if dropped from some height. The racket of the car was enough to bring out the people: aproned women, in their hands babies or sewing; lounging men in black caps, who only permitted themselves to look askance. The driver stopped and shouted for directions, addressing them familiarly as *compare*, and exchanging knowing glances at the expense of American visitors.

The Via Margherita was too steep and narrow for the cab to climb. A solid woman in black stood waiting at the bottom, children at her skirts. Pia approached her haltingly, as if she still had her sea legs, then took the woman in arms. While the driver unloaded, men gathered but stood back, responding to Nino's aloofness. The old man had unbent himself slowly from the car, his glance pausing for a moment on each face before sweeping to the next. Nino's eyes didn't rest even when the driver came up and began to speak to him.

"I have five children, mister," he said, the last word in English. "My company takes the money, and what do I get? Enough to feed them one day, two, if we can find the food. My son —"

Nino continued studying the new arrivals. It was impossible to tell whether or not this preoccupation were genuine. Eventually he paused in his survey, counted off some bills, held out his hand to the cabbie, and again looked away.

"It's what we agreed on," he said, still blindly, when the driver objected.

"Must I go on my knees to you?" the young man demanded at last.

Now Nino turned fully toward him, looked him up and down as if he were of new interest. "On your knees?" he repeated.

Although the air was filled with the noise of neighborly greeting, of bystanders calling out American addresses from Utica to Flatbush Avenue — though, beyond that, the cabbie's ears seemed to roar with his own shame — he distinctly took in, from Nino's words, a tone unheard before. Whatever of blasphemy or pride, of insult or bitterness Nino had uttered in the past hours, nothing he had yet spoken had sounded with this naked avidity.

The cabbie looked at the hawk-beaked old man as if he had just made a disgusting proposal. Then he told the American what he thought of him.

"Also to you," answered Nino, eyes gleaming, and again took up his search.

2

"**M**ust we sit here all day?" demanded Nino. "I'm stifling!"

He was pinned beside the stove in a corner of Pia's niece's downstairs room, which served as kitchen and parlor and sleeping-place for her two youngest. Pia sat opposite, adjacent to the washtub. Their countrymen stood between them, for want of chairs: a few distant connections — the widowed niece Menuzza and her offspring the only blood relatives remaining — and a larger number of the simply curious.

It had never been Nino's practice to disclose himself to strangers. But in this press he couldn't hear what Pia was saying, so he was compelled to answer their questions if only to counter her presumable idiocies.

Had he ever thought, one asked, to see again his native place?

"Only in hell," Nino replied.

Of course, another hazarded, because he could scarcely bring himself to part with the comforts of his American life?

"Comfortable, certainly," said Nino, "to break one's back in digging the gas line, and to be spat upon by the rich for your pains."

Trying a different approach, one asserted that his own father had been a friend of Nino's.

"And watched him starve, no doubt," Nino answered, rising to his feet. "Enough! I'm going out."

Until then, his *paesani* had succeeded in weaving Nino's unruliness into the fabric of civility. But he had finally stopped them. Silence overtook not only the men, but the women on the other side of the room.

"Where would you go, *Signore?*" It was Menuzza, speaking as hostess. Her aunt was already Zu'Pia to her, but she knew better than to risk such familiarity with the uncle.

"To the piazza," Nino answered, heading for the door.

"His mother's house was there," Pia explained.

Nothing more natural, everyone agreed, and followed Nino out as if they had been invited. The wife had seen her birthplace — the house that was now Menuzza's — so why shouldn't the husband be eager to see his?

Nino took little notice of them, though they continued to hem him in, down the narrow street. He spoke only when one observed that in the piazza he would of course find the church as well, where he had been married.

"Yes, also the prison," said Nino.

Apart from that word, he took no notice of them, although his eyes continued to wander restlessly, as if to take in the features of Pia's part of town. This had never been familiar to him. He had first set foot in it only two weeks before leaving for America, fulfilling one of his last duties. His family had come to be beholden even to creditors of the order of Pia's mother. By that time, there was only one currency in which the Zammataros could redeem a debt to a house of so many daughters.

But Nino showed less interest in the buildings of Pia's district, their peeling paint, their doorways open for light and air, than in the figures peering out. He examined each face with the extra attention one might bring in trying to determine not only what it was, but what it had once been.

As they turned out of the Via Margherita, the roadway broadened. Then the houses began to improve a little, displaying wrought-iron balconies, or decorated tiles set into the plaster. The last transition was more sudden, as the street gave way to the cobbled expanse of the piazza, where a high campanile, though in plain brown brick, towered on the right. Nino didn't look up at it. Rather, as he passed the church, he was regarding the largest house in the piazza, with a front four windows wide — a baron's house, long before the time of any now alive.

"That's where my husband lived," Pia said, pointing a few doors down from the four-windowed house, "before he grew poor."

On the great door of the baron's house hung an iron knocker, at a mildly careening angle. Nino's gaze was fixed upon it as he asked no one in particular, "And does Gianni Leoni still live there?"

Just then Menuzza, who had stopped before the church, called out, "Angelina! Let us in!"

From around the church's corner, a bucket of water in her hand, appeared a woman with a fine, high-cheekboned face, to which her wrinkled skin clung tightly, like an expensive upholstered chair that has lost its stuffing. As she fished a large key up from a pocket in her apron, she said, without turning to face Nino, "Yes, he lives there, but he's not home. He's making his rounds."

Nino swung around to look at the wizened woman, with a stare that sought to burn away falsehood, tell a lie from the truth. After a moment he said slowly, "Ah! So he still collects his loans, and lives as well as ever." His eyes were shining, as if it hardly mattered that the joke must now be against himself instead of another.

He must have felt something beside amusement, however. For when someone took his arm where he stood, saying, "Come along," Nino made no more objection than a doll, but permitted himself to be dragged after the others into the darkness of the church. He stopped inside the door, refusing at least to be taken further, though already in closer proximity than he ordinarily permitted himself to any altar.

Pia knelt before the crucifix, then stood looking up, in the dim light, at the paintings and statues. "But this I don't remember," she said, gesturing to an arc dotted with light bulbs that rose above the cross.

"Unfortunately, they don't work," Menuzza explained. "The soldiers" — she omitted to mention, as all the same to her, whether these were Germans or British, Italians or Americans — "took the machine, and it's been years since they've been lighted."

"So it's a lie, then," Nino said — he too was looking above the altar, but didn't appear to see — "that he's poor."

"Who?" asked Menuzza.

"That banker," Nino said, still looking at the arc.

"Gianni?" Angelina, the woman with the keys, turned to him. "If a dog in the gutter is poor, so is he. If it's his house you admire, let me tell you that there's not a table in it with four good legs, nor does it matter, since there's little enough food to put on top of one."

"*Povero!*" Pia sighed.

Nino, however, seemed to return to himself at these words. As they walked back into the piazza, Pia whispered that he should give a tip to Angelina, apparently the sexton of the church.

"Why take the place of God," her husband answered, "who rewards all virtue?"

They were conducted next through Nino's former house; the mayor, who lived there now, had invited them in. But Nino's only interest was in talking to Angelina, who seemed to know the most about Gianni. He kept up his questioning as they continued their excursion. At Pia's request, they were on their way to the graveyard on the other edge of town.

Nino was just asking on what resources Gianni lived, when Angelina stopped and said, "Ask him yourself."

Looking in the direction of her pointing hand, Nino saw the back of a man entering a low doorway. Shooting his hand into the air to stop the others, Nino followed after.

From the doorway he recognized the smells of a sick-room in the days before hospitals. On a mattress barely raised above the floor lay a figure shaking all over in what must be his last illness. An old woman, seated in a chair with her arms clutched before her, rose at the sight of this new visitor.

"So you thought to cheat me by dying, Gianni!" Nino said.

A man turned to look at him — not the man on the bed, but the man who had preceded Nino inside, and was now bent over to present his ear to the lips of the dying one. He had to look up at Nino, for he was on his knees.

Nino took a breath, as if to inhale the sight before him and incorporate it into his blood. The kneeling man was little older than Nino, with more hair remaining, though its unkempt thinness made him look all the more pathetic. His lower lip hung flabbily loose, trembling as if it had caught the dying man's disease. His pasty face didn't have much beard left to shave, and his eyes were unable to hold their gaze in any particular direction. He seemed to be living in fear for his life, unsure where the final blow might come from. He was barely recognizable, but Nino soon deduced the history of Gianni's form: he must have gone to fat in middle age, and now had declined without returning to that fairness of feature he had inherited from his father along with his riches.

Nino felt himself tremble, too, but took firmer hold of himself, and spoke.

"Are you trying to wring gold from this skeleton, then, Gianni, or have you been reduced to begging?"

"Yes, to begging," Gianni replied in a hoarse voice, his eyes meeting those of Nino — whom he didn't seem to recognize — only for a moment. "To begging for mercy."

"Mercy?" Nino repeated. "And of those you once made beg it from you?"

"Of God," Gianni said, looking down. At the same time, as of its own volition, his right hand rose to point to the water-stained ceiling above them.

"You think He'll answer?" Nino inquired. "Perhaps you would be more readily answered if you begged of me." Nino thrust his hand into his pocket, meanwhile moving back a step from the doorway, for the convenience of spectators in the street.

Gianni shook his head, trying a little smile; but his lips, unused to this position, soon relinquished it. "If it's money you'd offer, I'm afraid that's not for me. But the church would be happy of it." And he turned back to the deathbed.

Nino's hand froze in the motion of removing something from his pocket. He stood silent a moment; but if his effort were to keep a certain impatience from entering his voice when he next spoke, he was not completely successful. "And will the church feed you, Gianni?" he demanded.

Gianni turned to answer, but not with defiance. His face showed nothing but sorrow, weariness, regret. "My beloved friend, with the only food" — Gianni paused to wipe his mouth, as if it had watered at mention of the word — "that will avail."

Then, once more, he gave himself to his prayers.

3

"They say he found God in the prison," Menuzza explained to her visitors as they took the path to the *camposanto* outside of town. She held not only Pia's arm, but Nino's as well: after Gianni's last word, her aunt's husband had seemed to turn to a statue, and Menuzza had had to urge him away.

"And I suppose it's true," she went on, "for he spends his time going among the poor. Besides, what else was left to him? He lost his money in loans to those crooks in the government, who are no better now, and then he went to prison for what he had done for them. He wouldn't live today if the priest hadn't given Angelina the job as sexton. I've heard she takes in laundry, too, for those who can afford it. My mother told me his first mistake was trying to follow after his father, when he didn't have the stomach for it."

"Angelina?" asked Nino. It was the first word he had spoken since they left the dying man's den.

"Yes, that woman you spoke to, she's his wife," Menuzza replied. "And don't think there aren't people happy to see her cleaning up their dirt. But who is it easy for these days? My husband gave his life for his country, and think of the lousy pension they expect my children to live on! Even a healthy man, if he wants to work, must go as far as China."

By this time they had come to the low stone wall defining the cemetery, and Menuzza held her tongue. Pia found her family's graves without direction. Nino followed with Menuzza, scarcely looking around him, though he had laid both his parents to rest here. Instead, he said, with half a laugh, "It's a joke, of course."

"*Signore?*" Menuzza inquired.

"This *porcheria* about Gianni Leoni and God," said Nino.

Menuzza looked at the old man, hardly believing he had spoken such language in such a place. But his lower lip curved in disgust, as if he had bitten into dirt. Possessed of a mind of her own since well before her widowhood, Menuzza might have answered, elder and guest though he was; but just then she caught sight of Pia, at her mother's grave, bringing her hands to her face and beginning gently to rock.

Menuzza went to put her hand on her aunt's shoulder. She held it there until Pia at last stood up.

"Filomena was a good woman," Menuzza said. She had been named after Pia's mother.

Pia showed her a face that was strangely tearless — but looked as if it had seen a ghost.

"Are you all right, Zu'Pia?"

Pia simply shook her head. Then, as they walked back, she returned to the earlier subject.

"That poor man," Pia murmured, "he was a true son to his father, to stay beside him even after death."

The words were not too soft for Nino's hearing. "And if I'd stayed in this hole," he demanded, "who would have fed you, tell me? Isn't that why your mother sold you to me?"

If such remarks did not create the best first impression in the minds of his hosts, it was still observed with approval, the next morning, that he went immediately to visit Don Giuseppe. What clearer sign of charitable intentions? The priest's mission on behalf of Pianosanto, financed by some American *paesani*, had moved Nino to take his trip, as everyone knew from Pia's account.

"And who would have expected such good of him?" Pia had asked, meaning no satire of her husband, but only praise of God's ability to transform the most obdurate.

Yet Don Giuseppe did not succeed in bringing up from Nino's pocket the rubber-banded roll of bills that had been seen when he paid the driver. While the priest spoke feelingly of the needs of the church, its falling plaster and loose bricks ready to tumble at any moment upon the heads of the worshippers, Nino only wanted to know about Gianni Leoni.

Yes, he was a good man, who did far more than his Easter duty, Don Giuseppe affirmed.

"But you know what he was before?" Nino asked.

"In the eyes of God, what does it matter what one was before?" the young man replied with some impatience, perhaps thinking of his own far-off hill town, and his city education; he felt rather exiled in Pianosanto.

"The ladies of Boston have paid for an entire set of vest-
ments and altar cloths," he added.

This noble example, however, had no influence on
Nino.

His townsmen were no more successful. Coming to
Menuzza's house in rusty vests — one day the son of his
compare, another a distant cousin by marriage on his
mother's side — they brought Nino to witness sights likely
to inspire generosity. But in homes where invalids lan-
guished unsuccored by medicines, where stoves stood cold
and larders empty, Nino only remarked that, as he understood it, poor men were no longer fond of money. Intro-
duced to a boy of fine prospects, if someone would only
pay his apprenticeship, or to a girl whose marriage was
delayed by the question of a dowry, Nino advised them
that it was wiser not to start with too much, lest they end
up dressed in rags, as some other men had been known to.
Even lesser appeals went unanswered: once, when Nino
had placed his order in the *caffè*, the owner had gestured
to the men at the other tables, and hinted at what was
expected of an American visitor; but Nino let his solitary
order stand.

Soon enough, the visits of his *paesani* ceased. A few
still defended him, suggesting that his gifts might be waiting until the *festa*; hadn't he talked first to Don Giuseppe?
Or perhaps, American though he was, he had no money at
all. Hadn't his wife said that her children had paid for the
tickets? Hadn't she herself, for all her fine clothes, been
seen cleaning in Menuzza's house, as if to work out her
board?

In fact, however, Nino was not universally close, and
the hint about Menuzza, in particular, was unjust. That
lady had succeeded in opening Nino's hand, by the simple
expedient of ignoring what was sometimes called his wit.
The very first evening, after she had led Nino, grunting
with the suitcases, to her own upstairs room, he had

turned to her and said, "I suppose you'll expect money for our keep."

"I won't say no," she had replied, and named her price.

It was true that she was somewhat embarrassed by the heavy work Pia took on, beginning the day after her arrival, and did what she could to stop it. But she saw in this no reason to lessen her exactions from her aunt's husband.

Nor was Menuzza the only person who could bring Nino to spend. Early in his sojourn, as he was being shepherded between hovels, Nino had run into Gianni in the street. Stopping him by a touch on the shoulder, Nino had said that he would be willing to give his dirty clothes to be cleaned by Gianni's wife.

It seemed — as Gianni eventually explained it, amid stutterings and grateful nods and pointless half-smiles — that his wife had informed him she could take no more.

"Speak to me later, *Signore*," a man nearby quietly remarked to Nino, who was watching the banker's retreating back, "and I might find someone for you."

Without even looking to recognize the man again, Nino dropped the subject entirely.

The next week, when the visitors had stopped coming, and Nino's only escape from Menuzza's brood was to sit in Enzo's *caffè*, Nino belatedly took up the owner's hint.

"Drinks for all!" he suddenly announced.

Eyebrows rose; Enzo nodded approvingly; but the men had too much dignity to acknowledge his favor more openly.

Still, Nino spoke as if in response to their gratitude. "I know that, to some, the touch of money is painful," he said. He was looking over at the counter, where Gianni Leoni — who had entered just before Nino's announcement — stood consulting Enzo about some matter. "But who could refuse a man his drink? And let there be bread, too, Enzo," he added, "for I understand that is eaten even in church."

A chair scraped at Nino's side, and he glanced over at the novel sound.

"Manfredo Pasquale," said a scrawny, unshaven, and tieless man, extending a hand that was not received. "Didn't I tell them, I had never seen so generous a face? Ah, that man comes and goes like a ghost."

Nino looked puzzled for a moment, then suddenly swung his whole body around. It was too late: Gianni had disappeared.

"Your drink, *Signore*," said Enzo, having crossed the room to serve Nino first.

But Nino didn't touch his glass.

This made some of his fellow drinkers uncomfortable. But Pasquale evidently felt a friendship established, and picked up the thread his countrymen had dropped. Undiscouraged by Nino's lack of interest in his tubercular wife or ragged children, Pasquale regularly seated himself at Nino's table, and even came to Menuzza's to fetch him once, on the day of the weekly market.

"What *disgrazia!*" Pasquale exclaimed as he stood with his new friend on the edge of the piazza, looking at the cheeses and winter vegetables, at a slender selection of factory-made stockings and shirts and kitchen utensils.

"So much to buy, and no one to buy it!" Pasquale cupped his hands before him, in expression of dismay, perhaps also of a receptive spirit.

Nino began to make his way between the carts, Pasquale sociably at his shoulder. Occasionally someone offered a greeting; but Nino didn't trouble himself to reply.

"To think," Pasquale exclaimed as they passed an old clothes stand, "to think of a man so rich he could throw out a coat like this!"

The fur-collared top coat hung alone, as the stand's specialty. Nino stopped to take a sleeve between his fingers.

"Did you see," said Nino — his first acknowledgment that he was not alone — "the rag that man had on for a coat?"

Pasquale didn't trouble himself as to Nino's meaning, saying instead, "Remind yourself, *Signore*, that there are enough who have no coat at all." And he stroked the vest that was the sole barrier between his own shirt and the morning chill.

This effort was fruitless, though Nino bought the coat. Still, Pasquale didn't leave empty-handed.

Nino brought up a coin up from his pocket and said, "Find me that banker, that Leoni."

Although unused to running errands like a boy, Pasquale consented with an eye to ultimate profits. In little time he returned, attended by the shambling Gianni.

"You have offended me, Gianni," said Nino.

"Oh, what have I done, *Signore?*" Gianni asked. He had looked baffled at first; but Nino's question seemed to place him on familiar ground. His question in return was spoken not defensively, but only to speed his atonement. "Please tell me, and from my heart —"

Nino stopped him with a raised hand. "It is your coat that offends me," Nino said, with a sort of smile. "And the only way you can make it up to me is to take this one from my hand."

He held it out, with ritual decorum, so that those who had noted the impressive purchase might now look on with heightened attention.

Gianni stood blinking, as if Nino's words were a cloud of gnats about his head, threatening to fly into his eyes. He considered for a few moments, then began repeatedly to bow and nod as he spoke his thanks.

Nino stopped him, and said that the thanks he wanted was to see the coat worn here, in the piazza.

Again Gianni paused, then assured Nino that his wish would be met.

Now Nino turned over the precious cloth. Now he closed his eyes and breathed deeply as if he had just emerged from under the sea. Now he opened them again — to discover Gianni, that unstable candle, once more gone out.

"Where is he? Thief!" Nino cried, shoving Pasquale aside. His shouts brought some attention, though when people heard the story, and recognized the teller, they grew skeptical: how could an American possibly be robbed, possessor of that magic horn eternally replenished?

Soon enough, a woman called out, "*Ebbene*, stop your weeping, here's your coat." She was pointing behind him.

Nino spun around. Gianni's velvet still hung in limp, long-used folds from his shoulders, the sleeves still separating at the seams. Then the new coat appeared: not at its best, it was true, for it was too large for the wearer's form, and dragged along the ground each time his bad leg bent beneath him.

"Calm yourself, *Signore*," someone said, gesturing to the limping, slack-jawed figure beneath the coat. "Pippo doesn't have the wit to steal your coat, he must have mistaken it for his blanket. Isn't it true, Pippo?" The man bespoke Pippo with the exaggerated sweetness required to cajole a child or, as in this case, a halfwit. Then Nino heard the first laughter.

"Give him a kiss, my Pippo," said Gianni.

It was as Pippo came nearer, to show this sign of gratitude, that Nino turned and fled — though not before he heard someone ask, "What's happened?" and another reply:

"Don't you see? The idiot has found a brother."

4

Nino having disappeared from sight, Pasquale went looking for him at Menuzza's. But he had to settle for the wife.

"Didn't I tell them, *Signora*, that your husband had the most generous of faces?"

He stepped around Menuzza, who had until then blocked the door with her body, as if to bar entrance to this bedraggled visitor. But she seemed to have thought better of it. Turning to her aunt, she said, "Now that you have a guest, Zu'Pia, you must rest and let me finish."

She reached a hand out to Pia, who was scrubbing the bricks of Menuzza's floor with a wire brush.

But Pia waved her away. Menuzza gave up, and sat down to her sewing again.

"He's only waiting, it's what I've told them all along," said Pasquale, seating himself as well. "Besides, didn't he treat them all to wine? And now, look at what he's done today!" And he told them of the gift Nino had made to Gianni.

Pia's reply was to nod her head repeatedly as if for penance, saying "He's good, he's good," and scrub all the harder.

"It was Gianni he gave it to," Pasquale went on, "whatever you hear. Pippo only got it because that one doesn't know how to be glad of a gift, and passed it on to him. And now the idiot has a coat, and look what I must wear!"

"If he's come to beg of you, Zu'Pia," said Menuzza, "he's the one who should be on his knees. Now come and sit down."

But Pia kept at it, while Pasquale said, "We know better, don't we, *Signora*? Just as we know that your husband won't be satisfied with giving a coat only. If you ask

me, it's the *festa* he's waiting for — wouldn't you say?"
There was a little more uncertainty in this last question.

"What, *Signora?*" he added. Pia had mumbled something.

"Perhaps we won't be here then," Pia repeated, a little shamefacedly.

"*Che?*" asked Menuzza, putting down her sewing.

"Surely you're staying for your Madonna's feast — especially with the gifts you'll be giving that day," Pasquale skillfully added. "Don't you want to see her stop at your window, with the band? Perhaps you'll even be permitted to keep her in this house!"

"No!" Pia cried in sudden distress.

"But you must be joking, aunt," said Menuzza, smelling a rat, and privately naming it Nino. "You said you wanted to see the *festa.*"

"No, no," Pia repeated. She waved both her hands as if to stop all talk — though the fact was, she could scarcely hear them any more, in her fear of the very idea of staying for the Virgin's feast. She had looked forward, once, to witnessing that great event in her native town. She had looked forward, too, to seeing her mother's grave; but that sight, when it was vouchsafed, had taught her forever the folly of such wishing.

She had nurtured the wish every night at sea, kept awake by the awful rocking, the sense of being uprooted from all foundations. The rocking seemed to have gone on always, as if it had started before they embarked in New York. And so, she had begun to see in those wakeful nights, so it had: in forty years in America, she had never taken a certain, secure step. She had tottered like a child, even when she had become a mother herself. America had remained a maze, and when her children had gone out of sight, whether to walk to school around the block, or to move to suburban homes reachable only by car, it was as if they had dropped off the end of the earth and she could only pray for their safe return.

When she had reached Pianosanto — so unchanged from the landscape of her dreams, she could hardly believe she was waking — her *paesane* seemed instantly to understand her condition. Beginning with Menuzza's, one pair after another of welcoming arms had encompassed her as if to hold her up. But after a lifetime of perilous wavering, only one embrace could steady her.

Arrived at the graveyard, she had fallen to her knees among the tender weeds before her mother's stone. She was sure the warmth of the soil would penetrate the layers of her coat and skirt and cotton stockings. But she felt only coldness — not absorbed from the earth, but radiated from her own body. As if in death, the cold spread out from her heart to touch her fingers and toes. When she tried to distract herself from the freezing by uttering a prayer, the only words that came were those of a devil. They said: "Why did you send me away? Away, to become a stranger to my neighbors — to my blood — to myself?"

She grasped for other words within her, but these were all she could find. She thought, This is my mother, but she saw only gray stone; and she herself was just another.

She didn't dare speak aloud, lest these thoughts find voice. She couldn't even cry out that she was possessed, because it wasn't true. Cold creature of stone, she had possessed herself.

From that time, she could hardly look anyone in the face. When Menuzza had raised her to her feet, Pia could only think that her niece had no idea what monster filled her arms. In the following days, even as she helped in Menuzza's house, she had worked half in fear that she might somehow be sewing bad luck into the seams she mended, or stirring poisons into the *minestra*. She was glad that Nino alone held the purse strings, for if she had had gifts to offer, who could say what curses might have accompanied them unawares?

She went so far as to claim stomach aches on Sunday, like a naughty child, to stay home from Mass; not simply from doubt of any forgiveness, but from a hesitation to be seen by the eyes of Christ above the altar, and His mother in the niche to the side. That was why she had started at Pasquale's mention of the *festa*, when the Madonna was brought through the streets. She remembered, as a girl standing before this very house, watching the holy statue pass through the Via Margherita, blessing even families burdened with as many daughters as Filomena's. Pasquale's words showed the folly of thinking to evade those all-seeing eyes by the pretense of indigestion. He was too hopeful, of course, in expecting Nino to offer such a gift as would bring her to a special stop outside the house: unaccountably generous though Nino had been, any church would be the last to receive a dollar from him.

But the Virgin would require no more than a moment's peek in passing to see all she needed through Menuzza's upstairs window.

"Not stay for the *festa*? It's a sacrilege!"

So Pasquale was saying, when the front door opened. It was Nino, red-faced and winded.

"*Che fai?*" he spat out — not so much at the sight of his wife working while Menuzza sat idly by, as at the sight of the spy Pasquale.

"Who sends you?" Nino demanded.

His voice brought Pasquale to his feet, maneuvering to get between Nino and the door.

"Is it Gianni? Is it that priest? Do you think my years in America have made me forget," Nino asked, as Pasquale backed towards the street, "how to wring the chicken's neck?"

The next instant, amid sputterings of regards and respect, Pasquale was out the door.

"Am I to thank you, *Signore*," Menuzza asked after a moment's silence, "for driving away the guests I've invited to my house?"

Nino, who had been looking out the door after Pasquale, turned to face her.

"Forgive me," he replied, "if I thought I was doing your will. What else does a woman want but to drive guests away, who charges them to sleep on a broken bed, then makes them her slaves?"

He pointed to Pia, motionless on her knees. As if reminded of her duty, she bent once more to her task.

"Stop!" cried Nino, flinging a hand towards her.

"Really, *Signore*," Menuzza said, "she's not at your command."

Nino turned back to her. "I thank you for pointing out to me my errors," he said with a tight bow. "And if the sight of them offends you, I assure you they won't do so much longer. I find the smell of this town overpowers my breathing, and I must leave."

"With pleasure," Menuzza replied, answering his bow. "Only I want to know what tales you've been telling my aunt about taking her home before the *festa*. You said yourself the tickets were for May."

"As if you didn't know it already," Nino observed, "when you've doubtless put your fingers to everything I own. But to spare you the trouble of breaking more locks, let me tell you that I've just been to change the tickets" — here he pulled a slip of paper from his pocket — "and we leave for Palermo tomorrow."

"Tomorrow!" Pia whispered.

But Menuzza didn't hear.

"I knew it!" she cried, almost leaping up to stand at Pia's side. "You're taking the poor woman from just what she came to see. That's what she meant by saying she'd miss the *festa!*"

This was the first Nino had heard of Pia's notions. Even in the fury of sudden resolve and ready action that still kept his heart racing, he was a little disconcerted by his wife's eager consent.

"Oh, but he's right, we must go!" she urged. "If we leave the apartment empty too long, the landlord might rent it away from us. And who can say what will happen to the pension? And I've told you my daughter Agnes is expecting in the fall, and what if we're kept here by — by a war, or *qualcosa?* And the communists, Menuzza —"

Nino didn't wait to hear how the communists might inconvenience them. Before Pia could finish her sentence, he had headed up Menuzza's stairs to the bedroom. In bending to pull his suitcase from beneath the *matrimoniale*, he felt a sudden spike of pain in his back — the probing of that fanged instrument with which God had taken to torturing him in recent years. But he ignored it, straightened up, and began to empty his clothing from Menuzza's wardrobe.

Soon enough, Pia came to keep him company, and to encourage him in his decision.

"You're right, Nino," she said, "if we leave now, we can go to Assunta's grandson's wedding after all, and then she'd know you'd forgiven him for breaking the wine press that time. And if there was more money you wanted to give to the poor *paesani*, Menuzza will hold it, or you can leave it with that man, the one you gave the coat. Oh!"

Pia cried out suddenly; at her last word, Nino had slammed the lid of the suitcase. In another moment, Menuzza loomed in the doorway; they had heard her rush up the stairs.

"What are you doing to my aunt, monster?" she demanded. "It's not enough you must take her away for the sake of that Gianni Leoni, but you must strike her too?"

At her first sentence, Nino had whirled to answer in kind; at the second, he paused.

Seeing her advantage, Menuzza said, "It is that banker, isn't it, who drives you away?"

"What are you saying?" Nino replied with a dismissive gesture; but she noted his refusal to meet her eyes.

"Because we don't fall dead when you throw your money in our faces — because this Gianni doesn't kiss your feet — is that why you're leaving?"

Nino was kneading his lips, as if to rehearse his answer. But Pia came before.

"Oh, but Menuzza," she said, "the landlord might rent —"

Nino didn't hear the rest: he had pushed past Menuzza out the door.

5

Once in the street, Nino paused. He had managed to sustain a conversation in human language longer than he would have thought possible: for he had felt that he might fly off from the earth at any moment, or his head explode in a thousand pieces. After a moment's rest, however, he took his way up the Via Margherita. When he got to the piazza, he skirted it, perhaps to avoid the crush in the market. From there, he headed out of town, in the direction of the graveyard.

He strode right past the *camposanto* without looking. (He had hardly looked at it even on that first day, when they had dragged him to it. Someone had pointed out his family's plot to him, thinking he must have forgotten where it was, since he was standing with his back to the stone. He had turned only for a glance. Surely, the onlookers thought, no prayer could have been spoken in that time, scarce long enough for him to observe more than the straggly weeds, some topped with flowers, that had covered the holy ground in the last few weeks. Nor had Nino's face appeared much more beatific when he had turned back.) He didn't stop until, passing the crest of a hill, he was out of sight of Pianosanto.

His quick march had felt good to his pounding blood, and it felt good, too, as he sat on a boulder worked

free of the soil, to kick away a nearby stone. It might even
have given Nino pleasure, in his state of mind, to uproot
and devour the tall grass around him, gnashing his teeth
upon it. But this he restrained himself from doing.
Throughout his life he had kept himself from enacting his
most savage dreams — perhaps for fear that, no matter
how it might have impressed the world, the enactment
would have left his heart unsatisfied; left it beating in what
was at last revealed as a universe of emptiness, where a
blow could produce no sound, a grasp could seize no an-
chor, a cry could meet no listening ear. That was almost
how he felt now, planning his departure from this place
where all men had sought nothing but to shame him. For
he was leaving them the victors.

He closed his eyes and let the breeze blow on his
face, the cool spring breeze that made the weeds whisper
as he sat in blackness. He opened his eyes again and
looked about him with the aimless interest of the man who
has lost everything. Some of the weeds growing out of the
rocky soil had blossomed. He recognized them as the same
flowers that grew in the *camposanto*; for he had looked
long enough at least to remember that.

In fact, it might have surprised those who had seen
him at the graveyard to know how many thoughts had
gone through his mind as he had stood there that first day.
They were memories of his father's deathbed, mostly,
strange and unaccountable memories, no doubt distorted
by a child's ignorance. (He was only eight years old at the
time; the family had endured twelve more, old Massimo
Leoni's dunning taken over by his young son Gianni, before they'd had to give up.) There was sadness in the
memories: Nino's mother was weeping, his aunt half-sing-
ing, beside herself with grief, a litany of those his father
was leaving helpless behind him. Yet the dying man himself, as Nino recalled it, was smiling at him, and saying
strange things.

"What are you crying for?" he asked, rubbing his hand on his son's wet cheek. "Have they forgotten our jokes, my Nino? Or perhaps," he said with a look of mock fear on his emaciated face, "your mother is angry because she doesn't like my flowers." But then he gestured to what belied his words: the vase where Donna Maruzza had put the flowers Nino's father had sent him to pick, with great secrecy, for her saint's day.

Perhaps they were the same flowers, again, that Nino saw about him today. Or perhaps not; a child's perceptions could not be trusted. But Nino was sure, at least, that they too had been no more than weeds, the only gift his father, by that time, could afford to offer.

And how much chance was there even for weeds in this hard country? In many places around where Nino sat, the stones had triumphed, making a bare patch. The weeds that had managed to survive had often been forced to struggle for every inch. Sometimes what had been one rock seemed actually to have been cracked in half, the matching edges now pushed apart from each other, by wisps of green. A miracle, Pia might have said, who saw miracles in a chamberpot. But if that evidence of battle told anything of God, it was only that He had arranged a world where even the strongest can be broken, a world in which no creature, great or small, is without the weakness that will destroy it.

At that thought Nino suddenly looked again at the rock, almost as if it had been in fact a miraculous messenger. No creature without a weakness: perhaps his mistake had been in not looking carefully enough. From the moment he had decided to visit his *paese*, his dreams and his waking visions had been filled with Gianni's white face. He had hardly thought of what he would do on encountering it. Since arriving, his acts had been ruled by chance, by accident — and that was what had given God his opportunity. Nino could hardly believe his laxness in having yielded such an advantage to this, his oldest enemy; perhaps it was old age.

But he was young again now, or at least certain of the steely hardness of the spirit that endured like the bones beneath his loosening flesh. He need only apply his mind to Gianni's condition as he had so far failed to do; must examine the banker's life for the fissure, sure to be there, though invisible to all but himself, that would give him the power to split the man in two.

Nino looked about him more calmly. His breathing grew less shallow. At last he rose, ready to return, and walked home with a steadier step. You might have thought it was the influence of beauty that had calmed him. The spring rains — of which Nino had taken note only in the extra twinges he felt each morning — had recently begun. They had washed off the dust, brought out green and new shoots, and left a glinting sparkle still on the blooming asphodel, so that you could understand why the Greeks had planted them in Elysium.

He rested surprisingly well that night, although for the first time in forty years he slept alone, on a pallet in the kitchen. Menuzza had insisted on taking back the double bed, that Pia might sleep with her. It was no more than she had done, she said, for her neighbor Santa, when Santa's husband had raised a hand to her. Although Pia had defended her husband against the slander, Nino did not object.

Next morning, he rose early from his pallet and went straight for the church. The door was open. Inside he found Angelina with her mop, doing her Monday cleaning.

The crone was halfway down from the altar. The floor was easy to wash, for there were no pews as in America: here you still had to pay for a folding chair, or advertise your poverty by standing at the back. She saw Nino come in, but hardly paused a moment in her rhythmic swipes.

"I have something to ask," Nino said at last, a little surprised to feel his chest tighten as he spoke to the washerwoman.

Angelina pulled her mop upright in her left hand, and looked at him. "I thought *you* were the one who had everything," she said, significantly rubbing the thumb of her right hand over the fingers.

Brutes though he knew these people to be, Nino was shocked at her barefaced demand.

"You require money then, if I only wish to ask after your husband's health?"

Angelina put her hand to her hip. "I'm surprised you're so hesitant to speak, *Signore*, of the only thing that enables you to come and insult your *paesani*."

"It's me that insults *them*, then?" He spoke with feeling, yet was able to keep from raising his voice.

"If you care for an argument," Angelina observed — wearily now, having realized there was nothing to expect from this source — "I'm not the one you require. To me, no insult you gave them would be undeserved. You might have thought that only among beasts could one whom people once respected — one they used to flatter and kiss — be kicked and spat upon, and thrown into the ditch, because he did what they themselves would have done if they only had the means."

"You complain," Nino inquired with a smile, "though they gave you this job from charity?"

"Charity, certainly," Angelina replied. "How many floors do you think I washed, when I was on the other side of fifty? Do you know, when I was a girl, my father sent me for a whole year to my aunt in Palermo, just to cultivate my voice?"

But Nino was indifferent to this news, and in fact it was one of those days when Angelina herself was tired of her indignation.

"As to my husband's health," she went on with a shrug, "it continues the same as ever, though I don't know how, since he hardly touches the food I set before him. He imagines, I suppose, he can become an angel here on earth if he gives up being a man."

"I'm pleased to hear it," Nino answered. "But his health, generally — is there never anything that disturbs it? What else is to be expected, after all, in a man as old as — as that one?" He unconsciously held out a hand as if to seize any hint, even if offered only for the blink of an eye.

Now Angelina studied him. "What is it you want to know?"

"Only what I ask," Nino said. His words were reasonable, but he was growing a little impatient. "I'm leaving soon, and, for the sake of old memories, I would like to give him a particular gift, and I want to be sure it's nothing that would cause him pain — nothing resembling something he used to treasure, for instance, that might remind him too well of his loss."

Angelina lifted her mop back into the pail, as if to continue her work. Before she did, however, she looked again at Nino and said, "So you set yourself to humiliate this man?"

"What do you mean?" cried Nino, raising a hand. Again he reined himself in. "Excuse me, *Signora*, but it seems to me that, in our past meetings it's me that *he* has sought to humiliate. What makes you think I'd want to give him another opportunity?"

Angelina shook her head and said, as if she had not listened, "To look at you, fool though you evidently are, I wouldn't have thought you were so foolish as that. How do you expect, *Signore*, to shame a man who has no pride?" Then she touched the dripping mop to the floor, and pushed in Nino's direction.

Nino stood speechless, chewing over his lips. The woman continued her mopping as if he did not exist, and — there was no way to deny it — he could not think of the words that would prove his existence to her. At least they were alone, he thought, fully recognizing the cowardice of such a consolation. Perhaps to flee it, he finally turned and walked out into the morning sun. Standing before the church, he took off his cap and rubbed his left hand repeatedly over his head, like a man who was lost.

"*Signore*," a hoarse voice called.

He looked up, and saw Gianni crossing the piazza toward him. At once Nino began walking in the opposite direction.

But footsteps followed, and again the call, "*Signore!*"

Nino stopped and turned to the haggard man, whose body quivered as if each breath were dragged over bumpy ground.

"There is no word you could say that I want to hear."

Gianni blinked, then said, "I wish to thank you for the coat."

"You do? You do?" Nino's voice rose, and he felt a rushing wind in his temples. But he made fists of the hands in his pockets, and held himself in check. "It's not easy to understand you, Gianni," he said, a syllable at a time.

"Ah, forgive me, *Signore*," said Gianni, eyes watering.

Nino looked about him. A few women and children were engaged at the fountain. Old and idle men stood outside the *caffè*, or sat on the bench outside the town hall. Once hungry for audiences, today Nino would have been glad if the earth had swallowed them up. He had not returned to Pianosanto to be seen chatting with beggars. Yet he could not pull himself away.

"It seems to me you have required my forgiveness a hundred times already," Nino said. "But I'm afraid I'll be leaving before you can make me forgive you a hundred times more."

"I hope," said Gianni with a vapid smile, "I hope at least you won't leave before the *festa*."

"*Festeggiare!*" Nino cried. "Is that all," he added in a harsh whisper — for his shout had drawn a few glances — "is that all anyone can think of in this place?"

"Forgive —" Gianni began, then caught himself at the forbidden word. "I mean, you know, Don Giuseppe has said that I could help carry the Virgin this time. It's because he's a good man," Gianni earnestly explained, "since of course I could afford to give nothing to the church. My wife works only for food, and coal, and oil for the lamp."

"Truly," said Nino blankly; Gianni having paused, perhaps expecting a response to these unusually extended remarks.

"I know it's more than I should have," Gianni went on, "and not only because of my poverty. But I hope it's a sign of God's grace towards me, his promise for the next life, where the wrongs of our first life are righted." Gianni paused again, as if he imagined that Nino might offer him reassurance on such a point.

Nino was silent, however, for a long time. When he did speak at last, he said only, "You're not joking, then?" His own expression was strangely somber.

"Joking?" Gianni asked with knitted brows.

Nino looked to his left — looked to his right — looked up and down, as if he were measuring the houses on the piazza. "Why should I be surprised?" he asked at length, of no one in particular. "What else should I have expected it to be?"

"*Signore?*" Gianni said.

But Nino, after standing a minute longer, did not reply, or even say goodbye. He turned on his heel and walked up to the priest's door, where he knocked and was granted admittance.

When Nino emerged again, a half hour later, young Don Giuseppe was once more reviewing his mental list of influential connections, who might arrange a transfer for him — so tired had he grown of the moral compromises demanded of missionaries like himself, in parishes unsoftened by manners, or much money.

6

"What's wrong, aunt?" Menuzza asked later that afternoon. "What did he say to you?"

Nino had returned home by then; soon after, Pia had made her slow way down the stairs, a hand before her mouth.

"He's emptying the suitcase," Pia replied, letting her hand fall to her side. "He changed the ticket again. Now he says we don't leave until the *festa* is over."

She dropped into Menuzza's only padded chair. Pia had never permitted herself to sit in it before.

The niece looked at the ceiling, as if her eyes could penetrate not only the plaster, but the thick skull of her changeable lodger. After a moment she shook her head, giving up the effort.

"Well, don't worry," she said. "He stays on the pallet."

Menuzza gestured to the brick floor. Then she looked up again to the muffled sounds of Nino's movements.

"I know the Virgin permits sinners to buy forgiveness," Menuzza said, half to herself. "But can he really believe there's money enough in the world to save one like him?"

Within days, banners were hung in the piazza, and oil lamps on poles stood ready to illuminate the night. The church itself was closed, to increase people's wonder at the decorations when they entered after the procession. It was rumored that there might be something new for this year's *festa*: why else had a crate arrived, addressed to Don Giuseppe, and requiring three men to lift it?

At this season, more people than Menuzza were reminded of the Virgin's legendary favors. Stories of feast-time forgiveness, mercies, and miracles made their yearly round, like bagpipers at Christmas. In gratitude for gifts or acknowledgment of penitence, the Virgin had cured lung-racking coughs, taught the lame to walk again, brought windfalls to the debtor.

Yes, such things happened in America, too, Pia acknowledged in answer to the questions of her *paesane*. When they were girls, Pia's own daughters had followed the procession, at the behest of her friend Assunta. Decked in white, they were part of the contingent of twelve virgins whose labor Assunta had offered up in hope of her son Sammy's early release from prison. It had come, too, and much sooner than thought possible: the very next week, Sammy was stopping by his mother's apartment for a hasty embrace on his way out of state — the Virgin, on this occasion, having worked through unorthodox channels.

But just as the Madonna in America was only a copy of the authentic one in Pianosanto — discovered by miracle in a cave years ago — so the native magic, Pia was reminded, was far stronger. Here, a young woman's betrayer, protected from punishment by his family's wealth, had brained himself in a fall the very night after the poor one's mother had accompanied the Madonna through town on hands and knees. And a man of remarkable devoutness who had had the misfortune to murder his brother — the victim being laid out on the day of the *festa* — had received the most startling of answers to prayer. As the Madonna had passed the family's house, the corpse had sat up to confess the truth to his grieving mother. Though his brother had been seen putting his hands to his throat, the skeleton explained that this organ was already constricted, thanks to the poison he had administered to himself some hours earlier. This incontrovertible evidence of suicide cleared not only the pious murderer's reputation but, still more importantly, his conscience.

The murderer's miracle so impressed Pia that, as she listened to Menuzza's sister-in-law tell it, she peeled an onion almost to nothing. She took the story to bed with her, turned it in her mind while Menuzza lay snoring beside her. Could it be possible — as she thought it, she scarcely dared look, even in the dark, to where the picture of the Virgin decorated Menuzza's bedroom wall — that there might be forgiveness also for one like herself?

She must offer, of course, much more than a walk in the procession, with her feet bare to the stones, and her head bare too. That would hardly be painful to her, who had passed her whole childhood without shoes, and who was only embarrassed by the hat Nino made her wear when she went out with Menuzza. (However it might be in America, in Pianosanto no one wore anything but a kerchief.) Nor could the gift be money: Nino had never let her carry any since the day, in America, that someone had relieved her of a dirty bill she had found in the street, explaining that cash in such a condition must be returned to the bank.

The question of a fitting sacrifice troubled Pia for some time — until the solution presented itself so suddenly, so easily, it seemed almost a sign of divine favor in itself. She was doing nothing unusual, only ironing the children's good dresses, just unfolded from the trunk. The task was far more soothing than she found it in America, for she heated the irons on the stove in the old way, rather than having to plug them into holes where electricity lurked — waiting, who knew how impatiently, to leap out at the unsuspecting. There was a similar comfort in all the work she did at Menuzza's, where you could launder without fear of a wringer that turned of its own cruel will, and sew undergarments yourself, rather than shopping for them as her daughter Agnes made her do, down a flight of moving stairs that ended in a sort of meat grinder. It was as she slowly stroked, feeling the cloth grow warm beneath her fingers, that Pia's answer came.

Although it was all she had, it would be little enough to offer in recompense for the boon she sought from Mary.

The morning of the *festa*, Pia Zammataro woke alone. Menuzza had risen earlier, to get her children ready. In the confusion of waking, Pia thought they were her own children, that she must tend to them. Then she remembered where she was, and who — and half wished herself asleep again.

But she made herself rise, and washed her feet with care, though they would soon be dirty enough from her walk after the Madonna. When she had dried them, she left the towel lapped over them for a while, as an uncertain bride, just arrayed by her friends, hesitates a moment before looking in the mirror, hoping she will be changed. Only when Menuzza called from downstairs did Pia raise the cloth. She looked away quickly, hurrying on her stockings and shoes — she would wear these in Menuzza's house, only removing them at the door — but she could not deny what she had seen. Old woman's feet, all bone and callus, toes twisted by American shoes. "Forgive me," she whispered, the first of ten thousand times that day, already convinced there was no forgiveness.

Nino had left before, possibly to find a spot among the watchers. Menuzza and the children accompanied her to the piazza in silence, respectful of her vow to walk the procession. Except for her clothes, Pia looked just like the other old women waiting outside the church, handkerchiefs already prepared for the Virgin's approach. She was not in motion yet, but waited just within the open door of the church, on a platform with four poles lashed to it. Don Giuseppe stood by with several men, among them Gianni and, as Pia was surprised to see, her husband Nino.

Don Giuseppe looked uneasy at giving orders to men so much his elder: he was hardly more than a boy. If Pia could have heard them, the words he spoke at last — in response to a nod from Nino — would have confirmed her impression of his boyishness. They were awkward and stumbling, like a boy's who has broken a window.

"I would have told you before this, *Signore*," the priest said. He was addressing Gianni, though he scarcely looked at him. "But it was his condition. You understand, *Signore* — I knew that — despite what I said before — I knew you wouldn't mind it. The true Christian cares only for the good — the good of his neighbors. And it's for the Virgin, you understand."

But Gianni didn't seem to understand. He looked on, in his weathered best suit, as if the priest were uttering blessings, though in a foreign tongue.

"So this man," Don Giuseppe brought out at last, "this man, for his great gift, must be given your place." And he pointed to the Virgin's platform.

It took the politely smiling Gianni a moment, as he looked from the priest to the Virgin and back again. But then his face froze, and in the same instant he let out a despairing, "But —!"

He said no more. It was a giving up of the ghost, and in the next moment Gianni had fallen in on himself, his head hanging, his shoulders bent forward: the whole man, in fact, looking only slightly more broken than usual.

Don Giuseppe directed the bearers to their positions. At that moment, Pia was not the only onlooker astonished to see one of the poles taken up by Nino himself.

There had been little display in Gianni's reaction. Still, it was something for Nino to carry in his heart as he bore the pole to his shoulder. Such distraction was fortunate, since from the moment he raised his corner of the platform Nino realized that, however great the Virgin's compassion was fabled to be, she clearly had none for men with sensitive backs.

Indeed, it might have been a question just how much the memory of Gianni's gasp lightened the burden that only grew as Nino walked their slow tread out into the light of the piazza, where those ready to cheer in praise of the Virgin, and those on the verge of tears with consciousness of their sins against her, were for a moment silenced at the sight of Nino in the procession. The silence soon gave way to speech, and it seemed he didn't miss one word as he passed through the piazza, beginning the statue's circuit of the town.

There was general surprise and occasional anger that Nino should have been allotted such a place of honor. By itself, the anger might have pleased Nino. But it was usually diffused by someone pointing out that Nino could only have merited this position, like the other bearers, by a remarkable gift.

"And it was long enough in coming!" someone complained upon hearing this argument.

"But at least it came," the speaker was answered, "and think of this: his ugly face will be gone, but we'll have the benefit of whatever it is he's left behind."

Some rude boys acted out their envy in cruel tricks: noting the rich American's grunts, they asked him if he didn't want help with his load, and walked beside him a few steps, their hands supporting an imaginary pole at their shoulders, their exaggerated grimaces mocking the expressions that found their way involuntarily to Nino's face.

But few were so hard-hearted. Pious, black-clad ladies along the way weepily expressed their pleasure that this man, once noted for his blasphemies, had as good as confessed his sins. For what else did it mean when you made so great an offering, as Nino must have, for the *festa?*

One of these ladies even approached Nino when the bearers paused, before the house of a special donor. It was a warm day, and she reached out a cloth to Nino's streaming forehead. But the American repelled her by a snarl that seemed to come, not from a man's throat, but from a beast's.

It took them well over an hour to traverse that Via Dolorosa, up street and down, out to the edge of town, then back to the center. When they had returned to the church, and propped the Virgin and her garlands of ribbon beside the altar, Nino refused the offer of a chair. He was no more able to bend enough to sit down than he could straighten himself to stand. He leaned against a wall, as the priest prepared for the Mass. It was here that Pia joined him.

She had walked unnoticed among the other penitents, though her husband, yards ahead, had drawn so much attention. She would have been hard to recognize in any case, so often had she raised her hands to her face to hide her weeping, to her mouth to muffle her sobs. Yet it seemed to her that these efforts were futile: the first beat of the drum, accompanying the band that played sad songs, had broken open her heart, never to be sealed again. She did not see the houses that she passed; the starts and stops of the parade made no more impression than the memory of a breeze. She forgot her vow — only knew herself exposed to the eye of heaven, a pain so penetrating it was almost like relief.

She did not remember until she was back at the church. She arrived hardly aware that she had moved. The crowd pushed her through the bare, high front into the darkness, where candles glistened like stars, and bunting draped the niches of the saints. She noted it all — yes, this was beauty — but no feelings were left inside her to marvel with. She had wanted to confess her worthlessness; she had done it. Now she was left with the fact.

She had hoped — so she realized, with shame — for a sign, for some pledge that her confession, and her promise, had granted her new life. No sign had come. If it had, most likely she would have been no more able to respond to it than she was able to appreciate the church's decorations. Her pilgrimage had left her scoured, emptied out, as she had been after her last child, and nothing, they said, would grow there any more.

At least she wasn't frightened to be here again, beneath the Virgin's gaze. Perhaps, after all, this was the Virgin's gift: that she might enter the church as freely, now, as any dried-up leaf, or piece of dust.

The stone floor was cold on her feet: Menuzza had brought her shoes, but Pia had not looked for her. Seeing Nino, she went to join him. She remembered that he had carried the statue, but without the astonishment she had felt at first seeing him take up his burden. Most likely it mattered little to the Queen of Heaven who bore her on earth, any more than men give thought to the life of worms beneath the ground. Pia had long given up praying that he might be changed — had learned to plead only that she might not be infected, spouses though they were, by the strange disease that turned him from all grace. But now she saw the presumption even of that hope. Mother, child, husband, wife — what were these to each other, for good or ill, but so many chance-blown leaves, bits of foam on the ocean wave, drawn together for a moment by the wake of a passing ship — though they spent their time in pleading or concealment, hopes and fears?

She stood next to Nino, where she belonged, hardly listening for the priest's first words. Before these came, however, there was a sudden communal cry. She thought at first they were under attack, for the racket was something between the roar of an armored tank and the firing of a hundred rifles. Then the cries of "*Grazie, Maria*" arose, as the lights of the arc above the altar, so long dark, burst into full glare, powered by the new generator that Don Giuseppe's acolyte had set going.

Someone whispered to Pia: "Was it your husband" — the word in their dialect was *cristianu* — "that paid for it?" "Of course, who else could afford it?" another affirmed. A third grumbled audibly, "It was the Germans that took it, and a worse than German that brings it back."

Pia looked at Nino. Almost alone, he paid no attention to the lights to which, if they spoke truly, he had given life.

"But Nino — was it really you?" she asked.

Still he made no reply, tired perhaps from his labors — or was it, possibly, from the unprecedented experience of being raised to heaven by the arms of the Virgin, inclining to her children?

Pia looked up at the statue of Mary, dressed in a fine new robe. Her head was bent eternally towards her suppliants, her hands held out to them. Was there a mortal creature who could say what she could not do?

At the thought, Pia was aware of another voice, speaking in her ear. There was a moment before she recognized it, so unexpected, so yearned for.

"What matter," it said, "what kept us apart — what error of mine, what change of yours, all forced upon us without our wish? Hasn't the past become nothing — can't each forgive the other — now that, at last, you're home?"

"*Madre!*" Pia said aloud. She looked about her: she was still in the church, still beside Nino. But the voice had been undeniable, she had heard it as surely as the outward sounds of the sputtering machine. Then she fell to her knees.

Only the motion of others, leaving the church when the Mass had ended, brought her back to herself. She heard the noise of the machine; she looked up to the smiling Virgin; and the fear that had prostrated her fell away. She stood and, taking Nino by the arm, walked out into the day.

For Nino had remained throughout the Mass, his first in years, simply from exhaustion. If he accepted his wife's arm, it was because he frankly needed her support on the walk home. When they arrived at Menuzza's, though he was unable to climb the stairs, he could at least manage to sit while the aunt and niece prepared the holiday meal.

Even from a seated position, however, Nino could speak with undiminished authority. So he did now, saying to Pia, "And if you spend the day in cooking, tell me, when will you pack your suitcase?"

Pia turned to him from the basin where she was washing greens. Her husband's voice was as harsh as in the old days, as if he still contended with the Virgin's saving force. But she could be patient now — or forever, as her promise required. "No, Nino," she gently replied, "I don't think I'll go to Palermo. You go without me."

Nino drew himself up — not without difficulty — in his chair. "Not go to Palermo?" he demanded. "And how, tell me, if you don't go to Palermo, will you get back to America?"

"America?" she repeated, a little puzzled, but still serene, and freely willing to explain.

"Oh, no, I'm not going there, Nino," she said. "I'm staying here."

7

Nino raised himself from the chair — a little too quickly, so that he had to reach out, as in affection, for the shoulder of Menuzza's ten-year old daughter, who was peeling garlic. He seized the hand back as abruptly as if it had touched the hot stove, then stepped up behind Pia.

"Not going? What are you talking about?"

"Ah! Are you surprised, Nino?" Pia asked, turning back to him with a look of sympathy that made him raise his hand. He intended only to place it on her shoulder in warning, but he was stopped by an equally threatening glance from Menuzza.

"Surprised?" he repeated, the hand suspended before him. "That you've lost your mind?"

"You understand," Pia assured him, with supernatural confidence, "it's the promise I made to the Virgin, if she would forgive my sins. It will be hard to leave the children, but after all, they're grown; and think of the years my own mother passed without—"

But Nino didn't let her finish. "The Virgin!" he cried — then added an epithet that brought Menuzza to her feet, wielding a bloody knife. (Today, at least, there would be meat on her stingy table.)

"Listen, Nino," she said, "remember there are young ones in this house."

"And how can I forget," Nino replied, "when they break my ears with their cries, and pinch me with their nails, blood of the devil that they are?"

But he was not to be so easily distracted as this.

"And what of your sins to your husband," he demanded of Pia, "leaving him behind?"

Pia was startled at his language — not as her husband's, since it was no more than what she was used to, but as that of the new man he had become. Still, she answered him as reasonably as possible.

"But, Nino, you could stay too, you know. Think of all your new friends here." She didn't say it, but he could hardly deny that, after a lifetime of sharpening his tongue, he had left few friends behind in America. "And your blood in the *camposanto*, Nino. And — and you can see those lights you bought for the church!"

"May they burst and burn that building down, and everyone inside it!" Nino cried. "We go tomorrow!"

"Well, then," Pia shrugged, not quite so confident of his understanding, but wholly unshaken in her resolve, "you go on without me." And she returned to her work.

There was a point at which even Nino recognized that speech became futile. He stood staring, after Pia's last syllable, until Menuzza remarked, "*Signore*, either move or hand me the roasting pan you see there." He stared at her in turn, as if she too were speaking the same barbarian tongue. Then, with a wordless cry, he made his way to the stairs and, gritting his teeth, climbed up to the bedroom.

He leaned on the *matrimoniale* for a while. It was one of those old, high beds such as he remembered from his youth. Then he bent down to open his suitcase, as if its contents would prove some larger point. Everything was there, and he was about to close the lid when he heard the sounds of conversation coming up from the kitchen. What were they discussing? The niece wanted to know if the aunt put sugar in her ricotta; the aunt thought the greens needed two hours of boiling.

Nino slammed shut the door to the bedroom. Hearing from the street the cry of a chestnut vendor, he shut the window as well. Then he climbed onto the bed, shoes and all, and arranged himself on his side in the somewhat curled position demanded by his back.

Though he didn't sleep, he lay there some hours. He wouldn't come down when they called him for the meal, wouldn't join them when they said they were going to see the fireworks. If he were capable of pleasure, he might have been pleased, not long after, at the sudden downpour clattering on the roof tiles above his head, and the ensuing muffled sounds of people fleeing back to their homes. When the women returned, he got up from the bed, feeling somewhat less crippled, and went downstairs.

Their good clothes were wet through, any satisfaction he might have taken in the sight being diminished only by their unaffected cheerfulness.

"I hope you've had some sense returned to you now," said Nino to Pia, who was unsticking her blouse from her bosom, "as dogs do when they're doused."

"So you're still in your vile temper, demon?" inquired Menuzza.

Nino answered only by a glance, then turned back to Pia. "You admit," he asked her, "that we're going tomorrow?"

"Why do you say that?" Pia innocently replied. "I told you this afternoon."

"Ah, yes, certainly" Nino said, nodding. "And what, then, if I go without you?"

"Isn't that," Pia asked, "what you're going to do?"

"What do you mean?" Nino replied, tossing up a hand at this absurdity.

"You've got the ticket," Pia reminded him, "and you seem so eager." She had been patting her damp forehead with a dishcloth Menuzza had offered her; but now she paused in order to shrug at this instance of masculine unaccountability, with which there was no sense in arguing. "I thought you were going to go."

Nino stared at her in silence for a moment. If his wife could shy at the most harmless of sights — a child playing mumbletypeg, for instance — it was equally true that she could maintain an unaccountable serenity in the face of the gravest disasters, and would no doubt have carried on her crocheting at the lip of an erupting volcano.

"And you would stay here," he said at last, "without me?"

"If you leave" — here she shook her head at his small grasp of logic — "what else can I do?"

"*Ebbene*," Menuzza broke in impatiently, pausing in her brisk rubbing of her children's arms and legs, "don't you understand what she's saying?"

Nino turned to her. "As for you, viper, if you think I'll break my back another night on your dirty floor, I must offer my regrets."

"Have you found somewhere better, then — where they'll take you?" Menuzza added, straightening up and flicking the cloth over her shoulder.

"And if I did," Nino replied, "tell me, please, what you'd do for the rent from me that you've been living on.

For I assure you I wouldn't pay a penny for this one." He gestured to Pia. "Tell me, are you ready to support her for her life?"

"And why not? Isn't she my blood? Now," Menuzza added with a nod of mock courtesy, "I'm tired, and I'm going to my bed. I suggest, *Signore*, that you go find yours." She pointed to the door.

Pia, too, had finished her drying, and was straightening out the cloth on its hanger near the stove.

"And you," Nino said to her — his breath was coming a little heavily now — "you let her put your husband on the street?"

"Well, if you don't like the pallet, Nino," Pia replied, showing the palms of her hands. "But are you sure, Menuzza," she asked her niece, with that malleability reserved for all but him, "are you sure he can't stay in the bed?"

But Nino didn't wait for Menuzza's answer. He strode outside, where the initial cloudburst had slowed to a steady, soaking rain, leaving the deserted streets to Nino alone. There was something to match his temper in the clinging moisture that soon enough dripped from his nose and eyebrows, and down inside his collar. Even without it, he would have been conscious of every inch of skin that held in his roiling blood, like the too-tight garb in which an infant is swaddled beyond all its powers of wrenching free. It invaded his eyes and ears, he breathed it as well, until his socks were so wet that he felt as if there were mud inside his shoes as well as out, his shirt so penetrated that he began to shiver.

He looked ahead of him for an overhanging roof, but the rain came aslant down the road, so that not even a balcony could protect him. As he approached the piazza, towards which he had headed without thinking, he passed several grander houses at which he might have knocked as people had done in centuries past, when hospitality was as naturally to be expected as the bandits who roamed the countryside. But something restrained him.

He found an unlocked door at last, left open all night on account of the *festa*, and he let himself in. The place was lit up, for though the generator had been turned off, that people might rest in peace, the thick candles still burnt before the image of the Virgin. Lying down on the stone floor, Nino pressed his back against the wall, made a pillow of his arms, and fell asleep.

8

Nino's dream became confused by the creak of a heavy door, the echoing of wooden-soled shoes on stone. When he opened his eyes to the gray morning, the church door was closing, and something rattled in the lock. With a sigh, he rose, but only to his knees — not from spiritual motives, but from his usual morning stiffness. The air seemed cold after the stones to which his body had lent its warmth, and his clothes smelt of the smoke from the low-burning candles. He stood upright; then, slightly bent, and as slowly as a man with a hangover, he walked to the door and pulled the handle. It was locked.

As he tried it again and then again, he began to remember the sound of those steps, began to wonder if someone stood just on the other side of the lock. He banged on the door, demanded its opening. When a voice at last answered him, it wasn't from the church steps, but from one of the side windows, which had been left open a crack.

"What temper in a man who's experienced a miracle!" the voice declared. "For I suppose you flew here in your sleep? Or was it love of your machine that brought you?"

He crossed over and was not surprised to see, her head just rising above the sill of the narrow window, shrivelled

Angelina. "Let me out," Nino said, with a look some might have found menacing enough.

Angelina, however, was not among them. "You want to come out, now? Oh, how frightened I am, of so brave a man, who chooses only the weakest on whom to exercise his strength. If I even thought of setting you free," she said, her tone changing, "believe me, it would only be so that you might see what you've done to that man." The voice that had begun in mockery ended in a passionate vindictiveness such as he wouldn't have thought the crone had energy for.

But Nino was not troubled, knowing a woman's vindictiveness, though violent as a trapped rodent's, to be just as futile. "And what could I have done," Nino asked her, "to a man you yourself told me had no pride? Now, shall I call out, and have you jailed for holding me against my will? Or is the prison a place so familiar to you it no longer holds any terrors?"

After a moment, drawing her lips still tighter in her prune's face, the woman thrust her open palm through the window to Nino.

"I could have guessed," he observed with a nod, "that this was what your principles would come to." He pulled out his pouch, removed a coin, and placed it in the hand, which closed upon it at once.

He went to wait for her by the door. When she opened it, he didn't trouble himself to look at her, but headed through the heavy air — the rain had left all its dampness behind — to the Via Margherita.

He refused to enter. When Menuzza's door was opened to him, he looked in, saw his wife, and called her outside.

But Menuzza had to come, too. Standing in the doorway, she gave Pia permission to meet her husband in the street, but with one condition: if she heard one sound that troubled her —. She did not specify the consequence.

Once she was gone, Nino turned to his wife.

"It's not every husband who would give his wife a second chance," he said sternly. "And even *my* patience is at its limit." He stressed the pronoun as if this fact were quite remarkable. "The bus is in an hour. Do you come with me?"

She gave him a sort of smile, as if it might please him, and said in her usual quaver — the effect neither of fear nor of shame, but of her age merely — "No, if you must go, I think it's better that you go alone."

Nino looked at her for the space of a breath. Then he said, "Do you know I slept on stone last night?"

"Ah, I hope you didn't hurt your back," Pia replied, as if he might have forgotten to check for the familiar throbs.

"Of course not, I did it because I heard that was the cure."

"Ah!" said Pia with generous interest.

Nino closed his eyes for a moment. Then he said, with enforced calm, "I mean what I said about the money, despite what your Menuzza tells you. If I go, you won't get a penny out of me."

"But you've forgotten your pension, Nino," Pia reassured him, placing a hand on his arm. "Menuzza says there are men even here who still get the money from America, so it will be there when you go home. You needn't worry, you'll have money to send." She offered him the sympathetic look she had mastered at wakes and funerals.

Nino pulled his arm away. The Via Margherita, from its top where laundry lined the horizon down to the bottom where you could study the rooves as conveniently as if you stood in the sky, looked no different from yesterday — no different, for that matter, from forty years ago. It seemed he had not moved a step in forty years: and what wall against his chest, what boulder in his way had prevented him, if not his wife?

"And how would you like it to be known," Nino hissed, "that you were a woman who had been left by her husband?"

"But what are you talking about?" Pia replied with unaltered placidity. "Isn't it how many women live? Think of all the years my sister Rosalia's husband was in Brazil! And Menuzza's husband, though he didn't cross the ocean, was always away at the mines. Who ever said a word against them?"

"Is that what it is?" Nino inquired. "Why, then, did you come with me the first time? Why didn't you let me go to America alone?"

"Because my mother made me go," Pia replied after a moment. She hadn't paused from uncertainty, but only from the wish to savor her reply. Her sad smile indicated the sort of emotion one brings to an old pain that has become, with time and understanding, a sort of happiness.

"Oh, certainly, of course," said Nino with a short laugh, "that's why all the brides run after the husbands."

"There you must be right." Pia nodded, as if he had made a good point. "At least in my own case, if my mother hadn't told me" — here came the sad smile again — "I certainly wouldn't have gone off with a strange man."

"What are you talking about?" Nino dismissed the subject with a wave, as too absurd for further thought. And yet, absurd though it was — was it Menuzza's voice, or one like hers inside his own brain, that cried out just then in awful triumph?

But Pia could not be stopped. "You see, Nino, I said to my mother, 'But why can't I stay here with you?', and she said —"

"I have no time for stories!" Nino suddenly cried, raising his hands — whether to seize her by the shoulders or to crush together the sides of his head. But he stopped himself, and merely repeated, his hands in fists before him, "Will you come, or not?"

But she would not.

"Then goodbye," he said, and spun away.

"But you're not leaving today?"

He turned back. "And what makes you think I would stay longer?"

"You've left behind your suitcase," Pia explained.

With a motion like a visible roar, Nino thrust past her into the house, made his noisy way up the stairs — paused to exchange a word with Menuzza, for Pia could hear her niece's voice — and hurtled back through the door, suitcase in hand.

"Goodbye, and kiss the children —" Pia began, reaching to offer the kiss she would send with him. But before she could touch him, he was gone.

Getting up that morning, Angelina had been surprised to find her husband still at home. He was usually gone by sunrise, that he might help old Paola out of bed.

"What, are you sick this morning?" she asked when she came upon him sitting by the cold stove. "I know better than to think you'd let yourself rest for any other reason."

"No, I'm not sick," Gianni had managed to say, though his voice sounded even to himself as if it came from the other side of the grave.

"I suppose you'll be taking the rest of the chicken to your beggars." She gestured to the shelf where the remains of their yesterday's dinner sat covered by a cloth. Don Giuseppe had given it to her, in honor of the *festa*. Gianni had made himself eat a leg to please her, though it's not so easy to swallow when your throat is full of tears.

"You might save me the carcass, at least, for soup," Angelina said, tying on her apron. She was about to leave for her work when something — perhaps the fact that he hadn't moved from the moment she had walked in — made her speak again.

"If you're not sick, then, why don't you get up, and go out?"

Gianni managed a shrug.

"What do you want, then?" she demanded. "Do you wish they'd kept you longer in jail?"

Gianni looked down and kept himself silent until, with a curse, she walked out. After all, wouldn't she be angrier still if he answered? Once before he had tried it — saying, yes, he did wish he'd been kept under lock and key — but the answer had driven the poor woman, whose temper had not been improved by poverty, to the worst fit of rage he'd ever seen.

Jail had been bad enough, surely, with the harsh treatment (not so easy to take for a man already old, whose bruises take longer to heal — one spot on his calf was purple still); with the language of the other men, and the hard faces of some of them, who looked as if they would eat you alive. But at night in the darkness, punctuated though it was by snoring, or when they were allowed into the courtyard and he sat quietly (right down on the grass, he had little shame) and looked at the sky, he had felt the first true peace in his life, knowing that here at least he could do no harm.

What else was the meaning of safety, after all? That the police had brought him to this asylum had been Gianni's first lesson in the miracle of forgiveness. Ever since, he had held on to his memory of those solitary moments as his dream of what the after-life was like.

But what vanity had led him to imagine he could earn his way to such a heaven? That question was what kept him motionless in his chair, what had kept him silent with Angelina during yesterday's holiday meal, what had restrained him from daring to seek communion under that lovely arc of lights, blazing again as in the old times when he had worn a clean shirt every day. It was as if, by keeping absolutely still, he might keep himself from sinning again, committing fresher and more awful crimes than those for which the Virgin was now punishing him. In the jail, he had at first been surprised when they took away his shoe-laces; but then he had been relieved, for who could say that he wouldn't have made of them some vile weapon?

It was that Nino who had stolen his place from him, Angelina had said when she saw his gloom at dinner. "Why should you give him the satisfaction of making you feel so bad?" she demanded.

But her words conveyed little meaning to Gianni, who saw the visitor only as a generous man, offering gifts to his *paesani*; and who, besides that, was one of Gianni's victims, too. In fact, Gianni couldn't remember the details of his offense against Nino, couldn't even remember Nino's family, so many different people had occupied the house he said was his. Gianni himself had owned it at one time, collecting its rents. Perhaps that had been after the death of this Nino's mother; for it had been one of Gianni's father's rules to accept a house in payment only if the owner seemed likely to vacate (that is, was undeniably in his last illness), since that cut down on trouble.

Gianni had always tried to follow these rules of his father, as a man walking with a load of dynamite in his arms recites to himself the laws of explosives. But when his father had died, Gianni, who was twenty-one, had at best an imperfect command of them. He had practiced faith-fully all he could remember: lend to these, a good family, never to those, a bad one; at the first late payment, send the clerk, at the second, go yourself; keep the city officials contented; show weakness, and you might as well slit your throat. Some might have said Gianni had practiced them well, too, for his very timidity used to harden his voice when he was required to be strict. Yet there came a time when he had grown only too conscious that the rules were slipping from him, or didn't apply — when there was no way to tell whose family was good, and city officials were changed overnight, when even counting twice to the same result seemed a task beyond Gianni's powers. Then his first son ran away; his second was killed in Africa; his daughter's husband took her to Argentina; his third and youngest son had visited the jail only to say that he repudiated his father and all his works. Think of the thousands killed, the young man had admonished the old one. And what else, in fact, could Gianni do, convinced as he was that he had as good as done it all? If they hadn't taken his shoelaces, might he not have killed again?

But in the end his jailers had sent him away, cast him adrift. And though he had turned to God for guidance, Gianni was as poor at keeping His rules as he had been at keeping his father's. When he thought he had earned forgiveness, his heart would teach him that he had not. And even when his heart was fooled, the world would give a sign, as it had done yesterday. Thinking he was so wise, he had failed entirely to guess what would please the Virgin, as a blind man might miss the hand stretched out to feed him. Who could say what task she had set him, that he had ignored in his benightedness? Perhaps Nino had been the opportunity that he had missed.

Gianni had sat through most of the morning by the time he arrived at this thought. When the sun at last breached the clouds, it was at its noon. Gianni was thinking of rousing himself, knowing how displeased his wife would be to return for the mid-day meal and find him in the same chair where she had left him. Just then, he heard a commotion in the piazza. It seemed to be voices calling, some in rebuke, some in mockery.

He got up and went to the front room. He looked out one of the windows, and saw what surprised him deeply: the very Nino he had been thinking of, but acting as if he had gone mad. While people stood about, commenting upon him, Nino knelt bellowing in front of the fountain, surrounded by what seemed to be piles of rags. It soon appeared that these were clothes, however, for Nino would take up one of the pieces — a shirt, say — and flail it about before throwing it, evidently with the intention of filling a suitcase that lay open beside him. But his aim was so poor, in his emotion, that as often as not the clothes would miss their destination and fall back onto the damp stones.

Gianni opened his door and stepped outside. "What is it?" he asked one of his neighbors, a woman holding one of her grand-children in her arms.

"Who knows?" she said. "He threw that up in the air" — she gestured with a free hand, evidently indicating the suitcase — "and it ended up everywhere. What did he expect, the madman? What did you say to him, Enzo?" she asked of the *caffè* owner, who had walked up to share his story with a new audience.

"I saw him standing there, waiting for the bus, one hour, two hours, and — well, you know how it is," he said, as they all nodded about what was to be expected of anything that came from out of town, whether a bus, a law, or a human being. "So I went out to tell him if it hadn't come by now, it wasn't coming today. But almost before I spoke — you'd think he was a bomb, and just the sound of my voice had set him off — he turned into a wild man!"

Nino had lowered his voice at last, and was muttering to himself the words with which he had been profaning the air. Still, the onlookers kept a safe distance, and few would have chosen to approach him at such a moment.

But approaching those whom others avoided was a task in which Gianni had become practiced in recent years. After Enzo's answer, Gianni crossed the piazza and knelt down beside the cursing man. Then, he began taking up one by one the clothes that lay strewn about, folding them neatly, and putting them into the suitcase. After a while, Nino paused in his own motions and sat back on his heels, watching Gianni.

At last he said, "What are you doing?"

"I'm putting these things away?" Gianni suggested, perfectly willing to take correction.

"And why?" Nino asked. "Once they're inside, where am I to go, who've been thrown out of my house and can find no car to take me from this hole?"

Gianni looked at him as if a statue he was praying to had suddenly made a gesture of love. "Is it true?" he said with wonder, as he would have said in that circumstance. But wasn't it his duty to accept what most strained belief?

"Oh, then, *Signore*," he said, reaching towards Nino, "won't you come to live with me?"

9

"It's only for one night," Nino was saying, not for the first time, as Gianni led him from the hall into the parlor. But Gianni couldn't have noticed the repetition, so eagerly was he himself speaking, as if Nino were in the market for real estate.

If Nino had in truth been a prospective buyer, he might perhaps have been excused for thinking the house, large though it was, a little cold and barn-like for human habitation. Not that it was in any way soiled or disordered: Angelina kept it as neat as she kept the church, whose austerity it somewhat matched. Surely, it was hard to feel at home in a parlor where — though the deep windowsills were lined with gaily painted tiles, and the floor was not rough brick but mellow-toned parquet — the windows were unsoftened by the drapery you might have expected in such a place, and the reflection of the sun on the polished wood was unshadowed not only by carpet, but by any furniture at all. Nino, had he given it thought, might have imagined the room had been emptied for a ball, except that so many of the other rooms he had been shown were equally bare. The furnishings had gone to the payment of debts, and presumably fulfilled them, since their shell, the former baronial home, had remained in Gianni's possession.

What was left behind was, as Angelina had implied, too battered to be desirable. These pieces had been put to whatever use was required. Angelina chopped her vegetables on a rickety gold-painted table that must once have served in some lady's dressing-room. None of the chairs were of the sturdy straw-bottomed sort that even Menuzza owned: one more spindly than the last, none matching another, their seats were upholstered in a variety of stained satins or velvets. Two beds had been left: the one in Gianni and Angelina's room, with a crack in its carven headboard, and a plainer one — perhaps it had once been used by servants — in what Gianni called the children's room.

"We keep this here for them," Gianni said, as if he truly imagined his children might rise again from the grave, from across the ocean, or from an enmity that put them at still farther distance from him. "I hope this will suit you."

"It's only for one night," said Nino, who was taking notice of very little that occurred outside him. No doubt this was why he didn't flinch under the touch of Gianni's hand, which was occasionally placed on Nino's shoulder — hesitantly, as if Gianni were grasping at a proffered gift he feared might be snatched back. If he had noticed, Nino surely wouldn't have borne it; though what exactly he would have said remained a question.

From the moment Gianni had first spoken to him, as they knelt before the fountain in apparent worship of water, Nino had wished to make nothing but harsh answers. He might have offered some telling remark about the effectiveness of the Virgin's protection; might have observed how even that lady seemed to be finicky, seemed hesitant to give her kiss of blessing to one so black with crime as Gianni; might have commented sharply on the appropriateness of Gianni's marriage choice, since the wife was evidently a thief as well as the husband. Yet the words

for these sentiments wouldn't come to Nino, long-prac-
ticed though he was in the insulting of benefactors, and
though he had decided to accept Gianni's offer (for he had
to sleep somewhere, and could not pretend even to himself that he had made many friends in this town). His
insistence on speaking only one sentence at least preserved
his dignity. But the fact was, dignity was not his motive.
He simply could form no other words.

Yet no very complicated thoughts occupied his mind.
Not for a moment, for instance, did he trouble himself
with his wife's foolish lies. He was only running through
his itinerary: he would sleep in Pianosanto tonight; tomorrow he would take the bus to Palermo — the day lost
didn't matter, he had already planned to allow a few days
for touring there; then the ship. That was all there was to
it, whatever stories his wife might make up in her effort to
keep him; that was all there was, and he would have left
her and her foolishness behind. Simple as the plan was,
Nino repeated it within himself over and over, as if he
were instructing a very slow child, or arguing with a recal-
citrant one.

These thoughts made him ignore not only Gianni's
touches, but all his solicitations. Once the tour of the
house was ended, and the two men had sat down in the
kitchen — the only room with chairs — Gianni offered his
guest a succession of things to eat and drink. But nothing
could bring Nino to speak.

He found his tongue at last, however, when Angelina
came home, shortly after noon.

That lady had been surprised more than once in her
lifetime: most particularly, perhaps, in the last six years,
when she had had to learn how to cook, how to wash,
how to mend, even how to do the man's job of handling
money, when there was any; how to endure the snubs of
old acquaintance, how to put on a submissive demeanor to
former servants of whom she required favors; how to keep
alive a husband who seemed ready to starve himself to get

more quickly to the heaven he aspired to. But few of these shocks had quite the suddenness of her discovery that, for his latest project in self-sacrifice, her husband had taken up Nino Zammataro.

She saw it at once, for Nino, sitting at her kitchen table, still held his suitcase in his hand. Since coming inside, he hadn't let it go, less from eagerness to run away, for which he showed no inclination, than from the sheer instinct to hold on to something, no matter what.

"And is it him now?" Angelina cried upon seeing Nino. "The wealthiest man who'll still talk to you, though it's only to insult you? Is he more worth your time than those sick ones who, though they spit in your face, have at least the excuse that their fevers put them out of their heads?"

Gianni didn't defend himself, simply looked at the floor. "And you!" she said, turning to Nino. "Have you run from your wife now?"

"If I have," Nino darkly replied, "do you think it isn't what every man's wife has given him cause to do?"

Although this was the first word he had spoken, his savage tone was apparently enough to silence Angelina, who made no reply. More surprisingly still, she made no further objection to Nino's presence. This last mystery, however, was explained later that afternoon. When Gianni finally left them alone at the call of nature — the only time he had left Nino's side — she turned to Nino and stated the figure she required for rent. The thirty *lire* was rather a bargain, being cheaper than Menuzza's price.

"It's only for one night," Nino said automatically, reaching for his money.

"All the better," observed Angelina. "And I hope you're not going to try to do worse than you've done to my husband, for you'll be disappointed, since there's no worse you could do."

"Yet you'd risk it," Nino asked her, for another moment called to himself, "for thirty *lire?*"

Doing worse to Gianni, however, was far from the chief thought on Nino's mind. When the banker returned with that same expression of desperate eagerness — the expression of a man given one last chance to plead for his life — Nino looked at him without special anger, almost without recognition. Even when Angelina made the dinner of beans and weeds still more unpalatable by her unceasing abuse of her husband, Nino barely took notice of him.

"You haven't touched your plate!" she cried.

"Ah, I'm not hungry," Gianni murmured, and then, a moment later, said, "Here, *Signore*, take some of mine," urging his portion on his guest, as if Nino were a needy child.

But Nino had scarcely sufficient presence of mind to motion away the eager fork.

By this time, however, it was no longer the itinerary that occupied him. Instead, he was mentally enumerating the thousand conveniences that would surely attend his visit to Palermo, now that the place would be untainted by Pia's company. Not only would he be free of the ridiculous tales she seemed to delight in inventing. Happier still, there would be no need to correct her, to keep her from losing her head amid the strange crowds and novel ways. He intended to dine out, and visit the most elegant spots, as he had had no time for on his arrival. Now, he would not be required — as he thought about it, it occurred to him that this was probably the greatest benefit — to worry about her shaming him before the residents, by her countless errors and oafish display.

He would wear his blue suit, and that would surely be proper; even if he didn't have a brocaded vest. Besides, he reminded himself as that involuntary thought threatened to lead him astray, it was forty years ago that he had observed those high-colored vests, worn by men parading in shiny black carriages. No doubt what elegance of dress remained was buried in the bombed-out ruins. And didn't everyone say they were starving there? What leisure would they have to give thought to clothes?

As to talking, he didn't concern himself for a moment; even if in America once (the memory now returned to him) a well-dressed man, who called himself a *Palermitano*, had heard Nino say something and looked down (the man had been tall as a scarecrow, who could respect such a man?) to ask him from what country he derived. And after all, what call would there be for Nino to speak — at least until he had had a chance to listen and imitate? There was bargaining for the hotel room, of course. But surely numbers sounded the same all over. And the hotel man might be dressed with the sort of shabbiness that had given Nino courage in addressing the cab driver.

Next morning Nino woke quite early, having changed his mind to the black pants. Once he had put them on, however, he changed his mind again. By the third change — for he had the room to himself, and what can't a man freely do in his privacy? — the sun had barely showed its head. There were two hours left before the bus (supposing that it came). He had said his last goodbyes, had even told Angelina and Gianni he might not see them, as if he imagined they could stay in bed until nine.

The prospect of waiting, however — either out on the piazza, to be greeted by countless wellwishers, or in this room, where a suitcase stood ready to supply him with equally numberless changes of clothing — suddenly seemed unappealing. Instead, leaving the suitcase behind, he strolled out Gianni's front door, and, for lack of other destination, made his way to the Via Margherita.

He had come to say goodbye, he remarked when Menuzza opened her door.

"Again," she observed, but without too much malice, since he was attired like a civilized man and had spoken, too, with something approaching civility. Why, after all, should a traveler on his way to meet his equals in the most important city of Sicily be anything but cool?

Early as it was, Pia was wearing her apron, and had her sleeves rolled up. She greeted Nino by saying, "We're doing the wash," and pointed to the pots heating on the stove, as if this more than anything else were what made the day remarkable. But she wasn't wholly oblivious, for her next words were, "So you go today, Nino?"

Nino nodded a little stiffly, taking a chair though none had been offered. In fact, his hostesses hardly had the politeness to keep their faces toward him. Pia at this moment, was talking to her *nipotina*, asking her to strip the beds.

"Your own grandchildren, no doubt, will miss your instruction of them," Nino observed, though not in the tone he usually reserved for argument; rather, as if it were merely a fact that had just occurred to him.

"Ah, when do I see them?" Pia replied, shaking her head a little regretfully as she leaned over a pot to take the steam on her face. "Once a month, twice. Besides, what do they understand of what I say? And what help are they to their mothers anyway, in school all the day? I think it's ready, Menuzza," she added, and the two women poured the pots of water into the tub waiting beside the stove.

Nino sat silent as they did it, and then as Pia took a knife and scraped off flakes of soap. The grandniece returned with the sheets and pillowcases, piling them at Nino's feet.

"All your pots and pans," Nino remarked, again as if it had merely happened to occur to him, "what will become of them?"

"The ones in America, you mean?" asked Pia, whose heart was evidently confirmed in its new citizenship. "The children can use them, I'm sure. Or, wait — since you're going home, won't you need them, Nino?"

He looked as if he might have been about to say something else. But after a moment he only agreed, "Ah, certainly."

Another silence followed, after which Nino inquired what she would do if she got sick, for he didn't know if there were doctors here. But Pia was able to reassure him that, just last winter, Menuzza's little Saredda had had the things in her throat removed.

The conversation proceeded for some time in this halting fashion. Now and then Nino consulted his watch. Eager though he was for his coming freedom, he did not permit himself to be moved to any rude hastiness of speech by the passing minutes. Even Menuzza found nothing to object to in his demeanor, for she did not speak once, except to make some comment to her aunt upon the task at hand.

The longest pause occurred about the time that Nino should be leaving, a circumstance that he marked with the words, "Well, it's time for me to go." He offered them three times, in fact, with some minutes' pause between each announcement. After the second repetition, he moved in his chair, as if to rise. Pia was in the thick of her work, joining Menuzza in wringing the moisture from a sheet back into the tub.

"Before I leave," he said, "I was wondering — I was asking myself — I wanted to know —." The sentences came halting; perhaps the triviality of the subject was such that he could not bring himself to speak of it. But at last he was able to finish his thought: "What was it you were saying, about the time we were married?"

Pia seemed puzzled at first, until Nino reminded her of their yesterday's conversation. Even then, more prodding was required before she would answer. One might have supposed shame of her old sin, though now forgiven, was what kept her silent. To be forced repeatedly to confess it, however, would only have seemed to Pia a just if not a pleasant penance. The truth was, she was simply slow to understand what he wanted to know, so unlikely did it seem that he should take interest in words of forty years ago, especially words spoken by her mother, of whom he had never had much favorable to say.

She hadn't wanted to marry, Pia began at length — but Nino cut her off immediately.

"And don't I know this? Wasn't I there to hear you say it?" His tone was suddenly harsh, and the change was so startling that Pia stopped, and went back to squeezing and twisting the cloth until he said, in a slightly straitened voice, "Very well, and what then?"

She hadn't wanted to marry, Pia began again; even if these words had offended Nino, she had never known more than one way to tell a story. She hadn't wanted to marry, though he was rich — "for so I thought you then," she explained, "since my family had always been so much poorer." But her mother had insisted, for how else was she to be fed?

"So I said I would," Pia continued, "but I asked her if I could stay with her after you went to America, instead of going to live in your mother's house. And my mother said I couldn't do either, but had to go with you.

"Well, as you can imagine, I didn't understand. What was there for me in America? Why should I want go to live among strangers? But my mother said if I didn't go, you would find someone else in America, as so many men did who left their wives behind, and then what would I live on? But won't you miss your bus, Nino?"

For all the urgency of this question, her husband was dwelling on her earlier remarks. "As you can imagine," Pia had said; and Nino, sitting in his best suit, occasionally jerking his head this way or that, offered a vivid picture of a man engaged in such an endeavor, as if he were trying to read, without dictionary, a book in an alien tongue. He said nothing for some time, listening to the falling rain of wash water. Then he asked, "And why, if I go back now, don't you fear the same thing?"

At this Menuzza laughed aloud. But Nino hardly seemed to hear. Pia, too, addressed the question as simply as if he had asked her for some common information, such as how to cast for the evil eye.

"But you're so old, Nino. And I don't know what woman could hope to please you with her cooking, since you like such strange things to eat."

Pia spoke these facts dispassionately, offering them as they occurred to her, without accent of complaint. Her husband appeared to listen in just the same spirit, his face a meditative mask. In fact, as he sat there he was waiting for the one clue that would make everything comprehensible. The mystery that confronted him proved somehow so compelling that, when the clue kept failing to present itself, he found himself craving more answers, and still more, with infinite appetite.

"And well-off though we are, you know, in America most men are richer still, and I would think the women would prefer those. And with your back, Nino — I don't mind helping you with your stockings those times when you can't bend, but a woman who hasn't known you before would probably think differently about it."

Nor were these the last of Pia's reasons, though others took longer to come to mind. Nino gave them the time they needed. Even when she seemed to have listed them all, and went behind Menuzza's house to hang some sheets, he waited in the kitchen. Although the bus was long gone by then, his patience was rewarded by Pia's returning with yet another thought. "And a younger man wouldn't have so sensitive a stomach, you know what *cicidi* do to you." Here Pia made a face, not in mockery, but in grave pantomime of the natural response to an unfortunate odor.

"Do you think your bus will have waited for you?" Pia asked when Nino at last rose to his feet.

"Perhaps," he replied, nodding his goodbye. But when he got to the piazza, he cast no look towards the place where it would have stopped.

"You haven't left, then?" asked Angelina, home for dinner.

"She asked me to stay another day," Nino replied with a shrug.

10

She had passed into her mother's life: there was no other way Pia could describe it. Until now, each day in the *paese* had seemed only a dream, too often a nightmare. But now that peace had come, the dream was all that had happened away from her home, in her other life, on the far side of the ocean. It was even hard to believe, at times, that she had made children, and that some of these had made children of their own; that she had lived several flights up, in a land where you might be knocked over by a streetcar at any moment.

There were days when she would take a walk, just for the pleasure of it, down alleys where her playmates had lived — long gone though most of them were by now — or out to the literal edge of town, a place where back walls bordered on a steep hill (though she refrained from rolling down it, as she had done in youngest childhood). Every day, without fail, she helped bring the water from the fountain. As a girl she had sometimes balked at the chore, not knowing then how rare a gift it is to walk on paths you've known from birth, hearing snatches of conversation in which you can understand every word, for the language is your own, and passing houses where, even if a mean man lived there, he knew your family and could direct you if you lost your way.

It was all the more like her girlhood life, perhaps, because there was no man to be troubled about. Not that she didn't see Nino, who visited every day. But he was no longer the bother men can be, interfering with those ways of doing things a woman has learned from her mother.

Nino's visits adhered to a predictable schedule, always occurring just when she was ready for a little rest after her first chore of the day; or, if he came while she was still busy, he didn't make her stop or get underfoot. There was almost a pleasure in them. He would sit at Menuzza's table without cluttering it with his jigsaw puzzles, as he had done in America, getting in the way of her work. Often his brow would be knitted, his concentration deep, as if he were doing one of those puzzles. Other times, he took on a distracted air, that half-frightened her, so much did he resemble in those moments men she had heard of whose spirits leave their bodies while they still live. There were other odd changes, too — she wondered sometimes if it was his age — in the husband she knew.

The conversations themselves, for instance: when had he ever asked her so many questions; or when, asking a question, had he ever stayed silent through her entire answer? The questions were about all sorts of things, from what she used to think about this or that, and what she thought today, to what she was doing just then. For he would watch her chores with an attentiveness itself unprecedented, and would ask about such things as why she was rubbing the ends of the cucumber together. When she had explained that it was to draw the bitterness out, he might then ask something else quite unrelated, perhaps what exactly it was that she did in the box factory, those years ago.

Now and again he would recur to the subject that confused her the most: returning to America. What confused her was why he was still here, though before he had seemed so eager to leave. One day, for instance, he asked her how she could think of fulfilling her promise to the Virgin with so little regret; how she could find it so easy, never returning to live out the life she had undertaken in America.

"In America?" she repeated. "But after all, Nino, does everyone stay? True, we were there for a long time —

but look at the LoSantos, they've been back for twenty years now. And don't you remember your friend Jimmy, the *Messinese*, how he left, oh, so many years ago? And all Menuzza's friends, their families had someone who worked in America for awhile, the same as people used to go away for picking or to the mines, you remember, Nino? But who would stay there? Do the *zolfatai* want to end their lives in the mine? And why — why should I want to end my life so far away from where my mother is buried?"

Nino was listening with his new attention, and Pia might have continued, but she was stopped by an uncomfortable memory. She had gone, a couple of days after the *festa*, to visit her mother's grave again, and this time her grandniece had accompanied her. "Let me show you something, Zu'Pia," the girl had said, motioning Pia to the little chapel at the edge of the *camposanto*. Before she got to the door, Pia knew what the child would show her, for in her own childhood she had been interested by the sight, down in the cellar, of the piles of bones, removed to make way for other graves. Pia peered down into the darkness, to please the child.

"Don't touch," she said, restraining the girl, who seemed ready to descend the stairs. They were heaped as casually as the stones she had seen in America when men were working on the streets, like the shards of discarded brick, when a building has been demolished, too broken to be used in constructing another. When she was a child, they had meant little more to her. But now that she had seen so many go under the earth — the large and hearty, the small and meek, the old, the young, all shapes and colors — she could only wonder that so much life had been put out, wonder when her mother would be taken from her place; when she herself, who had returned to be buried at her mother's side.

And what of her own children, when they came to find her? (For there could be no doubt that they would come, as she reminded herself each time she thought of them. Although this life, as Pia well knew, requires parents and children to be separated by oceans — although not one of Pia's friends in America had been present at the deathbed of both their parents — yet God at last permits the mother and the child — wasn't her own case proof? — to be joined again.) But what if they came, and could not find her? What if, when her own time came to be placed in her mother's arms, it was already too late, and Filomena was mingled hopelessly with those dishonored sticks?

Wasn't it as if there was almost no way to do right? Pia had thought that her error had been stepping on that first boat — that that uprooting had been the cause of all her sorrows — that, by undoing it, she had won back her lost peace. But if even your bones could be tossed aside —. She shook her head woefully, at God's strange schemes, and then, almost in the same instant, at her own questioning. She had no business to question; but she was too weak to do anything else in this place. She knew she ought to stay and grapple with her weakness. But though it might be cowardice, she took the easier way, and put the thoughts from her mind by gently bringing the child back into the sun.

Now, remembering it, she brought herself out of that darkness again, and, doubtless, just as weakly. For she said, "And after all, Nino, why don't you stay here, too? I think," she added, looking about — her niece was not in the room — "Menuzza would even let you back."

But she knew what Menuzza would have said. "What? You'd keep your husband back, just to make company for you? Didn't I send my own to the mines, when he had to go?"

Nino didn't seem to guess this, but neither did he accept her offer. Instead, the niece's name seemed to rouse an old spark in him, for he said, in that grim tone which was always somehow suggestive of enjoyment, "Believe me, where I'm staying now, I hardly know I've left her behind."

His words, enigmatic as they might be to Pia, had a clear enough meaning to himself. Strangely unmanned though he seemed to have become in his daily visits to his wife — listening in silence, responding not with a man's justified assertion of his superior point of view, but only with another question — when he returned to the house of the former banker, Nino always found one who could bring to his tongue the sort of barbs he had once sharpened for Menuzza.

Yet that one was not Gianni: it was Angelina.

It had strangely come about that the power that could make Nino's whole body tremble like a weapon held too tightly — for, in such moments, Nino himself became wholly a weapon — had passed from Gianni to his wife. Nino himself could hardly believe it. The second morning he woke up in the bed of Gianni's children, Nino wondered how he would bear to look in that man's face (even if the bed had been paid for by another thirty *lire* to Angelina). Perhaps it was that the face, closely regarded, had so little in common with the one Nino remembered: the one tightly drawn with the ruthlessness of the young who have never known anything but comfort, and have no experience of suffering such as they inflict. Perhaps it was that the prospect of visiting Pia again, and again — by that second morning, something in Nino foretold that he was doomed to return like a ghost to Menuzza's house, until the terms of some unknown curse were met — perhaps that prospect rendered him more sensitive to the present tyranny of the woman than to the past tyranny of the man. But the fact was, when Nino came out into the kitchen, and heard Angelina berating Gianni, it was her voice more than his that worked like a file against Nino's breastbone, a hot poker in his brain. So it continued from that day.

Not that Gianni could no longer enrage him, for surely he did: by gluing himself to Nino's side (he had given up his usual rounds, it seemed); by pleading with Nino to eat more, drink more, take up more space; by hampering Nino with unwanted gifts (a strap for his watch that looked and smelled like beef jerky, a scarf so rough it might have served for removing your calluses); perhaps most of all by his craven submission to his wife's abuse. But somehow these were mere cobwebs Nino could brush away, compared to the goading effect of witnessing Angelina's daily vituperations.

Not one day was free of them. The afternoon Pia suggested that Nino stay, he returned to walk in on Angelina upbraiding her husband, who sat looking at his open hands, as if these might provide the answer that would satisfy her.

"What has he done now, *Signora?*" Nino inquired. "Did he breathe in when he should have breathed out? Did he cough when it wasn't convenient, and perhaps wait a moment too long before kneeling at your feet to beg forgiveness?"

Angelina hardly glanced at him, merely flung out an arm in his direction as she continued to address her cowering husband. "Not only is this what you do with the money I give you — but you do it for him! Does he even want it, like your other beggars, will he thank you even as well as those ungrateful ones do?"

The cause of battle this time, it turned out, was a rabbit Gianni had brought home from the butcher's for their dinner. Since Nino's arrival, Gianni had also purchased a chicken and several sausages, at amazing prices in this time of want; more meat, too, than had passed his doorsill in some months. Angelina had given each offering a like welcome.

"How can you act like this?" Nino demanded of his host, when Angelina had finally ejected the two men from her kitchen.

"Ah, you don't like rabbit," Gianni dismally replied, as if he should have guessed it from Nino's pallid interest in all his other gifts.

Nino exhaled sharply. "I mean, fool, how can you let her tell you what to do with your money? Whose money is it? Can't you stand up to her?"

"Do you think I should?" asked Gianni, who could not provide even the satisfactions of an argument, so ready was he to agree to any opinion espoused by his guest. This time, however, he dared at least one word of near-resistance.

"And yet they say the man should protect the wife," Gianni hesitantly put forth, "since she has vowed to rest beside him in his grave."

"All I hear is graves!" Nino cried, opening his arms as if the piazza were populated with headstones. The men were sitting on Gianni's doorstep, for want of other seat outside the kitchen from which they had been driven. Nino's raised voice brought a couple of glances from other men lounging in the square, but these soon turned back to their own concerns. By now, Gianni and Nino had been seen so regularly in company that the fact had lost its interest as an anomaly. Besides, whatever opinions Nino had once expressed about Gianni, to the onlooking citizenry there was a certain sense in the companionship of two men who each had so little in common with his *paesani*. After all, once the war was ended, though the town's population had not significantly altered, every one of the many who had argued on the Duce's side had disappeared into thin air. And as for Nino's pride in his wealth, who among them, should he have attained it, wouldn't instantly have turned it all over to the Church, from virtuous hesitancy to offend his poorer neighbors?

"You talk like an old man!" Nino added in disgust.

"But isn't it what we are?" Gianni asked. "Certainly, it's said that, from the moment we're born, we begin to grow old —"

At this point — for he could detect the encroachment of the Catechism — Nino excused himself, and walked off alone, as he did at such times, as far as the hill beyond the graveyard. (He never paused at the *camposanto* — or, if he did, it was not for long.) Often he would go directly after a visit to Pia, as if the breezes that found their way there might clear his head of the fog that seemed to engulf it in that house where she was staying. For despite the sense of doom that had early overtaken him, Nino had several times attempted to say goodbye. He had set himself a deadline, wiring to change his ticket again. Yet once in her presence, he could not take his farewell, could hardly remember he had meant to. Instead, just as if he were in a fog, he gave no thought to far-off destinations, to what had concerned him yesterday or would concern him tomorrow; he only groped for a guide-post, any object in the murk that he might touch. So he asked his questions, with no grander aim than to gain some hint of his whereabouts. Not until he was released again into the Via Margherita would he remember, and — having gone to wire again — promise himself to make his move tomorrow.

When he felt especially befuddled he would take his usual walk past the graveyard. (The weeds still blossomed there, so primitive were these people; at least in America, mowers cut them down.) Once in the hills again, sitting on his boulder, he might in solitude encourage himself by thinking of the happiness — for what else would it be, and for his life's first time? — that would await him in his adopted homeland.

The peace of his apartment would no longer be disturbed by the constant invasion of visitors almost as foolish as Pia herself, nor would he be nagged by her into sitting through a hundred wakes and weddings. He could do his puzzles undisturbed; even the men who called themselves his friends were mostly the husbands of hers, and there was good reason to believe they would feel less free, once she was gone, to breach his solitude. Nor would he be interrupted by Pia's own comings and goings, her tales of miraculous novenas and the money she had thrown away on wise women: tales that made him redden in rage, and forced him to expound to her, for the hundredth futile time, the unreason of all her doings.

Pia gone, he might do his puzzles morning to night, in such a silence as he had known only once in his married life. This had been three years ago, when she had gone to the hospital for her gall bladder. Every night of that time, when he would come home from the visiting hours — rather late, for he stayed to the end — the apartment was as still as any man could wish, and the door had closed itself with quite a sepulchral sound.

11

The day after the fight over the rabbit, Nino once more sought out his rural sanctuary. Pia had informed him that morning that she had asked Menuzza if he could return. Menuzza had said yes, if Nino would promise to behave himself.

Even Pia appeared conscious of some gracelessness in this condition. "Ah, you must thank her from me," Nino replied, "for certainly there is nothing I would rather do than spend the rest of my life in this country, under her command."

"But you can thank her yourself," Pia assured him, "she's only just stepped next door, and should be back — but where are you going, Nino?" Though Nino had just arrived, he was already rising from his chair and heading to the door.

"Excuse me," he had explained, "I must be a little sick today: there's something stuck in my throat." Then he had bowed himself out, and retreated to the hills.

He sat there a long time looking at the sky, feathered with dingy clouds like a chicken yard; looking at the distant ridge where you could see, barely distinguishable from the hill on which they perched, the mud-colored houses of Malachina, Pianosanto's old enemy (the honest folk of

Pianosanto would tell you that the people of Malachina had a third eye at the back of their heads, to help in their thieving; they were so stupid they cooked their pasta in their chamberpots, said the sages of Pianosanto); looking at the poor soil, half rocks and half weeds, from which *Pianosantese* and *Malachinese* alike had scratched a hard living. Had he ever lived here? Or had he lived here always, the concrete-paved life of America only the illusion of a moment, like the spots behind your eyelids when you close them? He had observed the wandering minds of men on their deathbeds, calling for the mothers of their boyhoods as if all the life between had never been. Had it been, then? And, if it hadn't, who could say if the far-off, remembered days, too, were any more than several spots before the eyes?

"Spots," he uttered aloud. The word had the heart-sinking emptiness of all we speak in solitude. In the next moment, however, he was embarrassed lest he might have been heard, for he grew conscious of steps behind him. He turned, and saw Angelina.

Her breath was coming fast after her climb, the hair that had escaped from her kerchief was pasted to her forehead with sweat. Her hand still held an oiled rag she used for polishing the fixtures in the church.

"Have you seen my husband?" she said the moment Nino had turned, while she continued to walk toward him.

"More often than I could have wished," Nino replied. "Not, however, this morning, for —"

But Angelina cut him off. "Where have you sent him? Have you driven him away?" she demanded, coming to a stand. "Did you think you could hide from me? Did you think I haven't seen you come here to think up your schemes?"

For his part, Nino remained seated. "What have I done, you want to know, what am I hiding from?" It was almost amusing. "Believe me, I'm sure you'll find your saint washing the feet of the lepers, or some such thing. Why don't you go —"

She interrupted him again. "I've looked everywhere. He's never missed his dinner, even if he eats it only with his eyes, for he knows I wouldn't stand for it. Have you driven him away? Have you hidden him, too? Or is it something still worse?" She had to pause, not out of any remorse for her unjust accusations, but from simple short-ness of breath.

"I don't know what you're talking about," said Nino, "but I know that I have no duty to listen, so if you'll excuse me —" He rose, nodding as if to show her out of his parlor.

But Angelina didn't budge. "So you've killed him, then?"

The witch's eyes narrowed to hateful slits, as if she really believed it, and she spat out her words like an acid meant to sear his flesh. Nino had intended to say no more, but at this he drew himself up and replied, "And if I had, wouldn't I, of all men, have had the right? Wouldn't I have been justified?"

"Truly? And for what?" Angelina favored him with all her scorn. "For saving the world from so dangerous, so powerful a man as he? Or is it that you'd seek to change your place with his, as he is today?"

There was a moment's pause such as, in his youth, Nino would never have permitted himself in debate. Yet he soon enough won back his advantage.

"Certainly, defend him," he taunted, meeting her eyes again, "as if he mattered to you. But do you think to fool me? If you've lost him, the only difference it would make to you is the money you could get for him!"

"What are you talking about?" She pretended indif-ference; but he knew better.

"Is there anyone in your town who doesn't know there's nothing to you but your greed?" Nino asked. "And if he's gone, perhaps he's gotten some sense, and run away from you."

Angelina was silent for a moment. "As you've run from your wife, you mean?"

Nino shrugged, as if to say it was true enough.

"Ah, *Signore*, it's *you* who thinks to fool," said Angelina with a nod.

"Excuse me?" Nino asked, easily her equal at the game of politeness.

"But I hope you don't think you've succeeded," Angelina went on, "for there's no one who doesn't know that it's your wife who has rid herself of you. It's that, *Signore*, that everyone in this town knows. How you go to plead with her every day, and, when she won't come along with you, you get Turiddu to wire for you, to ask the ship if you can't stay a little longer, a little longer.

"You may turn away," she said — for Nino, in a rare display of feebleness, had actually looked back toward Malachina, as if he were contemplating seeking refuge there — "but it's true all the same, and I hope the thought brings you happiness. May you keep thinking of it as my husband, wherever he is, breathes his pitiful last!"

Finally she stopped. When Nino turned back, however, she was still there, catching her breath before she pursued her search, and he was able to give her an answer in tones as firm as always.

"I have no idea what the town knows, or thinks it knows," he said, stepping past her to take his own way down the hill. "But as for me, I leave your house tomorrow."

"And who will have you?" Angelina asked behind him. This question always seemed, sooner or later, to come to the lips of Nino's hosts.

He paused and turned to her for a last time.

"Perhaps that is a question for paupers like yourself, who must live on the charity of others. But I have my own house, in that country from which I have stayed away too

long." Then he continued on his way, returning to town —
without a glance at anything along the way, at any field,
any beast, any graveyard — and to the bedroom he had
paid for in Gianni's house.

His decision — for, if before he had felt doomed to
stay, this time he knew with equal certainty that his departure could not be stopped — had nothing to do, of course,
with Angelina's words, in which there could be no syllable
of truth. It had simply come to him at last that he had
submitted long enough to the whims of his wife. He would
leave tomorrow, and await in Palermo the first ship that
would take him.

His packing was already done: he had been living out
of his suitcase like a man on the fly, though he had been
more than two weeks in Gianni's house. He counted his
money, as he did each night before bed. It was as good as
his bedtime, after all, for he didn't mean to leave his room
before next morning, having no desire to see his hosts
again. He would say goodbye to Pia in the morning, for he
supposed he owed her that. This time he had no fear that
any force, in nature or beyond, could keep him back. To
rest before his trip, he lay down upon the bed, and con-
templated the paunchy, semi-transparent cherubs that had,
for more than a century, been exerting themselves upon
the ceiling at a nobleman's desire.

As it happened, Nino didn't keep his hermit's vow.
Late in the afternoon, an uproar in the kitchen indicated
that Gianni had returned from wherever he had been.
Nino's curiosity getting the better of him, he went down
to hear the story.

He found Gianni warming himself beside the stove.
It was as clear as if Nino had seen it, however, that the
man himself hadn't presumed to take that seat, but had
been pushed into it by his wife, for her convenience in
berating him. It was always hard, of course, to calibrate
degrees of dejection in Gianni's spirits; but the man was
bent over so nearly in half that, unless he were merely

suffering some ailment of the stomach, Nino felt safe in judging him to be at his lowest.

"So tell me this," Angelina was demanding when Nino walked in. "How did you get back?"

"And where have you been, *Signore?*" Nino asked. "Your wife feared she might have to turn to some of her old protectors, you know what I mean, if you didn't return."

Whether he knew what Nino meant or not, Gianni seemed to prefer his question, and explained, as he had just explained to his wife, that he had gotten on the truck that brought men to work construction in Enna. Once there, however, he had been turned away by the supervisor. This fact was not difficult to understand when you looked at the palsied old man, whose suit hung about him as if he had been through an illness. Had he even been young and hearty, who would have hired him as he looked today: hunted and haunted, running for his life?

"And how did you get back?" Angelina persisted.

Gianni shook his head, looked at his hands, and finally whispered, "The bus."

It might not have seemed such a guilty word, but Angelina was adept at ferreting out crime. "And you used your money for it? Or" — for when Gianni was silent, she seemed to guess that his guilt was blacker still — "what debt did you make to pay?"

"Oh, no debt!" Gianni eagerly assured her. "But I sold a man my rosary." He looked away again as he confessed it, for there was no denying the rosary was the only thing of precious metal he still owned. He had given up even his watch before it, preferring to tell his hours in this more old-fashioned way.

Angelina nodded as if it was just what she'd expected. "And why, *Signore*, tell me this, why did you make this foolish trip?"

Gianni was silent a while; and when he looked up to answer, he addressed not Angelina, but Nino. "I thought, from what you said, *Signore*, that it would please you more if what I gave was bought with money of my own."

Now Angelina looked at Nino too. She didn't nod this time, didn't move at all, but stared fixedly as she said, "I must be thankful, then, that there is one man with sense in that city. For it's only that man, I see, that kept you from murdering my husband."

Nino went back to his room again, nor did anyone call him out from it. Gianni was free to starve as he pleased that night, for there was no evening meal. But the spouses evidently found other topics to turn to the purpose of their misery, for Nino heard them — Angelina nagging, Gianni pleading — long after he had gone to bed. At length Nino thought he must be asleep, because the noise had ended. But he still felt the pressure of his nightcap against his ears, saw the strip of moonlight through the shutter, and knew that the argument must be over.

Shortly after, he became aware of a recurrent sound, coming not from the couple's bedroom, but from the kitchen below. It was a kind of moan, like the rubbing of a heavy door against a floor, repeated at slow intervals. He tried to put it from his mind, this new sound conspiring against his rest. But at last he got up and, in his stocking feet, made his way downstairs.

It was Gianni, still dressed, sitting at the kitchen table, his head enfolded in his arms. Periodically he let forth a sob that resonated in this little cavern.

"Gianni! What are you doing?" Nino demanded.

Gianni looked up, his face red and streaked with tears, and moaned louder, as if his motion had been a pain to him. Then he said, "Damned! I'm damned!"

"What are you talking about? Are you crazy? Go to bed!" said Nino, too impatient for argument.

"There's no peace for me!" Gianni cried, making no effort to conceal his weeping. "I can't pay back my sins to anyone — to you! And now even my wife — she's never — in all the years — she put me out!" At last he looked

away from Nino, as if this shame at least must be con-
cealed.

"And then?" Nino asked. "Can't you be a man?"

Gianni shook his head. "Ah, I'm nothing!" He began
to sob again.

"Enough!" Nino held up his hand. "How do you
expect anyone to sleep?"

For all his woe, Gianni seemed struck by this point.
He swallowed a sob, with a sort of hiccuping sound, and
sat sniffing with his lips shut tight. Now and then, however, they puffed out as if there were a series of small
explosions going on inside him. The sounds continued
even when Nino had turned away. After a moment, he
turned back again.

"All right, are you going to sleep now?" he asked.

Gianni seemed about to say yes, and then to fear the
risk of opening his mouth, for what he might let loose. So
he simply nodded, and folded his two hands in his lap, as
if this were the accepted posture for sleep.

Nino looked at him for some time.

"And are you going to sleep there?" he demanded at
last.

Still hesitant to take a chance on speaking, Gianni
shrugged as if to say, "Where else?"

"Very well," said Nino, as wearily as if he had just
endured a lengthy argument, and beckoning with his hand.
"But one sound from you, and you sleep on the floor."
And Gianni followed him out of the kitchen.

12

If his visit to his native town had hurled Nino in a hundred directions, forced him to twist himself this way and
that, it had not completely sapped his strength. That was
why, for all his new understanding of the glances that
brushed him as he walked to the Via Margherita, he could

keep himself from stopping, as a feebler man might have stopped, to explain.

"Yes, today I leave despite what you think," the weak one might have said. "Look and see if it's not true," he might have challenged the onlookers, "watch what path I take when I come away from that house."

But Nino passed the spectators in silence, content to let time alone reveal their folly to them.

When Menuzza opened the door, it's true, he was reluctant to announce, in words too familiar, that he had come to say goodbye. Yet he hardened himself to the task, and bore without flinching the punishment for his former waverings: hearing the news, Menuzza insisted she must stay in the room to witness so unique, so unrepeatable an event.

In fact, Menuzza could hardly have left in her current state. Her hair, no longer matted beneath her kerchief, lay long and wet on her dishcloth-covered shoulders. Pia was showing her, what she herself had learned on the boat forty years before, how to wash and arrange her own hair. All but the very poorest ladies of Pianosanto still patronized the *parucchiere*, even for their small daughters, the expense made affordable only by the infrequency of the visits.

So Nino's farewell to his wife was conducted under the eyes of a chaperone, and while Pia's own eyes, though offering him an occasional uncertain glance, attended primarily to her labors. Had she any messages for the children, he asked her.

Pia's fingers paused for a moment. Was she human enough, then, Nino wondered, to miss her flesh and blood? If so, she only permitted her feeling to express itself in the endlessness of the list of instructive admonitions he was to carry with him.

These were so many, and so trivial, that Nino immediately saw he could never remember them. They were little facts that must be known about the items she left her

children as legacies (the inside of the rolling pin leaked
pieces of rust into your dough; be sure to sift the flour, for
a family of strange insects had taken up residence in the
barrel); details of the *paese* of particular relevance to them
(her cousin Samuele had a carpenter's shop now, should
Rosalie's six-year old son keep up his interest in hammer-
ing; Comare Rosina had broken her only vase, and didn't
Agnes have two, one on each end of her mantelpiece?);
exhortations on the conduct of life (don't let the small
children swallow their teeth, lest they continue to grow
inside; if you visit the beach in summer, remember to go
an odd number of times, never an even).

Nino nodded in agreement to everything. Nor did he
once need to consult his watch. He felt the minutes pass in
his stomach, and knew in a place as deep within him that
there was no way he could possibly overstay his time. He
had no hope, if he had had the wish, of escaping his
predestined journey.

Acquiescent as he appeared, however, he eventually
showed he wasn't listening. For Pia was in the middle of a
sentence — about bread, it seemed to be, as if her daughters didn't buy it ready-packaged at the store — when he
suddenly said, "So you never wanted to come, then."

"To come —?" Pia asked, not understanding.

But Menuzza was wiser. "Is it that you still think of,
Nino?" she asked. Her hands lying in enforced idleness on
her lap, she seized her first opportunity to be busy again,
even if it was about another's business. "That she preferred
staying with her mother to going off with you?

"And what?" Menuzza continued. "Are women usually so eager to run after the men? Is that why the men
must court them so hard?"

"Oh, but Nino never courted me, Menuzza," Pia observed in justice to her husband. "We were married in such
a rush, he just came home with my mother, and the next
day she told me I must have him. You see," — her hands

paused for a moment — "that's how my mother could make her mistake about him — I understand it now."

When Pia spoke of her recent enlightnment, it was generally in a tone of otherworldly bliss. But today, since Nino's announcement, customary though it was, she was not quite herself. She seemed distracted, so that Menuzza had grunted more than once when a hank of hair was carelessly pulled. And there was something of dutifulness in Pia's reference to her new knowledge.

"What mistake was that?" Nino asked, the old fog creeping back over him. But he would keep it at bay, would ask no more questions once this one were answered.

"To think you were that sort of man — the kind that woos the women. That's why there's no reason to mind, now that you want to go back. Even if there were a woman who would take you, I know you're not the one to woo her."

As she spoke, Pia shook her head a little sadly. Perhaps it was a kind of regret at her mother's error, persisting past all forgiveness; perhaps she pitied Nino's incapacity; or perhaps there was some other cause.

"I'm not?" asked Nino, though it was a question more than he had intended. "Then what have I done these past weeks?" He swept his arm before him as if the weeks had been arrayed about Menuzza's kitchen. "What have I done but court you, yes, and in the eyes of all the world, coming to this house every day like a fool?"

Pia was no more impressed than usual by his storming. "But that's not what Menuzza meant, Nino. Courting is when — when you come with gifts — flowers and such things — and you say — oh, you know, the sort of things men say in courting." So Pia elucidated it.

"Interesting things they must be," Nino observed, "that would make a woman do what she didn't intend to. Perhaps I will learn them in America."

"Listen to that! He warns you!" Menuzza laughed.

But Pia, though she failed to join in Menuzza's laugh, still seemed unthreatened; and indeed, Nino's momentary bitterness of speech had passed. He sat watching silently for the last few minutes he could allow. Then he rose — spoke no goodbye — but stood still, this time, to accept upon his cheek his wife's last kiss. If her subdued looks indicated any regret at her decision, that feeling was still insufficient to make her alter it.

When he returned to Gianni's, he brought his suitcase down to the front door, then went to the kitchen, where he found Gianni at his usual station, curled over himself like some dying animal. Hearing Nino come in, Gianni did what he could to straighten himself. Nino hadn't slept at all the night before, not for any noise Gianni had made, but from the very sound of Gianni holding his breath in fear of waking his bedfellow.

"Tell your wife this is for her," said Nino, putting some coins on the table; in the turmoil of the day, he hadn't paid her his last night's room and board.

"Thank you, *Signore*," Gianni mumbled. Then, after looking dutifully at the money, he remarked, "Ah, so much! Why, it's as much as she has been giving me these past weeks!" His enthusiasm was a little pale, only that of a man trying to take interest in life for politeness' sake.

Nino, however, showed a somewhat more genuine interest. "What do you mean, these past weeks?" he asked, after a moment.

Gianni looked away. "Yes, it's true as you said, *Signore*, all I have is what she gives me, and shamefully I take it, even though she herself has so little. And there's no telling how she must have deprived herself to do it, for often she has nothing to spare at all. But ever since you've been here, she has given me this much every day, can you imagine it? And what good have I done with it?" Gianni, for all his effort to be brave, put his hands to his head, and let out a sob. "In the sinner's fingers, even gold —"

Nino had listened intently, though the sentiments were such as sometimes made him rave. At the last sentence, he interrupted the miserable man. "Tell me, where is she now?"

Gianni wiped his eyes and said, "Ah, you want to say goodbye. She's doing the wash for Don Giuseppe, I think."

Nino scooped the coins from the table, nodded to Gianni, and walked out.

The priest was out, perhaps performing some of the duties Gianni had once taken off his hands. Angelina herself opened the door to Nino. She made no move to invite him in, but stood in the doorway, her apron wet, her sleeves rolled up above her elbows, her face in the sun a network of wrinkles like the rivers and streams of an immemorial landscape.

"I wanted to give you this." Nino showed her the coins.

"All right," she replied, letting him put them in her hand, which she thrust into her apron pocket. Then she waited for him to leave.

But he stood there unmoving. At last he said, "Why do you give this money to your husband? I mean, all the money I have given to you?"

"What business is it of yours?" she asked, putting her hand on the priest's door as if to close it.

To stop her, Nino put his own hand upon it. "If you give it to him, why do you complain of how he spends it?"

Angelina almost smiled at his stupidity. "And what good has it done him, tell me, spending it for you?" Then her smile was gone, replaced by her old scorn. "If you wanted to bring him low, *voi*, you may congratulate yourself as you leave this town."

She stepped back. Now Nino had to take hold of her arm to keep her from escaping him.

"And why didn't you keep my money for your own wealth? You who used to cultivate your voice?"

Angelina was silent, looking at him and then at his hand on her arm. Old crone as she was, and sweaty with work, her look suggested the dignity she must have known in former days. It sufficiently conveyed that Nino might trust her to stay if he let go — and that certainly she would speak under no other condition.

He released her.

"You've seen him, when he thinks he can do no good even to someone else," she said. Her voice now seemed lower and fuller, as if it, too, had not forgotten its cultivation. "Would it agree with your stomach to watch him like that, for days on end?"

"And if you'll throw your money away like this," demanded Nino, an urgent issue appearing to depend upon her answer, "why were you so angry for his seeking to earn more, or spending what he had for a trip on the bus?"

Angelina shook her head.

"I'm old," she said, though at this moment she looked younger than Nino had yet seen her. "What do I know but giving to him? Soon I'll die, and won't know even that." She spoke without bitterness, without pity.

"And if he won't take what I give," she went on, "isn't he telling me it's no difference to him — that I might as well go into the grave today?"

Her eyes met Nino's frankly, leaving him free to contradict her if he would. He held her gaze for a moment, though it wasn't easy for him. Then he nodded — his question answered — and turned away from her.

He crossed the piazza, admitted himself to the baron's old house — no mere knock could have roused Gianni from his chair — and sought out his host once more.

He stood in silence before him for some time, until Gianni himself asked, "Didn't you find her, then?"

Nino nodded, was silent another moment, and then said, "Gianni, what will you do when I leave?"

Gianni essayed a shrug, but even his shoulders would not obey him. Then he looked away, as if no answer were necessary. What can a statue do, after all, but sit unmoving where its maker has abandoned it?

"And will you obey your wife?" Nino asked.

Gianni looked at him, evidently to gauge, by Nino's features, the answer he desired. Did he mean to mock the husband's subservience? To counsel him to the sacramental fidelity pledged before the altar? The question was too hard.

"I don't know," said Gianni helplessly, and watched without surprise as Nino looked away, as much as saying, "What can one do with such a man?" "What, indeed?" Gianni might have answered.

"Very well," said Nino at last. "Then, will you obey the Virgin?"

Gianni looked up, his head trembling, whether with palsy or with unbearable longing for the answer to his own eternal question. "But how can I, *Signore?*" he pleaded.

Nino held his hand out before him, one finger extended in admonition. "When you sit down to a meal —" Nino began.

But Gianni could not contain his eagerness. "Oh, what, *Signore?*" he asked. Was it some new prayer for grace?

Nino closed his eyes, and took a breath, as if to give his words their fullest force. Then, looking gravely at Gianni, he said, "You must eat what is placed before you."

After Pia had finished, she sent Menuzza to sit in the sun to dry her hair. "I'll join you in a moment," she said. Then, after stopping to compliment her grandnieces on their sewing, she went upstairs to her bedroom.

It was the hour of day she had grown accustomed to spending with Nino: he had come earlier than usual this morning, on account of the bus. Since her operation, it seemed that she needed rest after being on her feet for any period. Nino's visits had always been a pleasant enough way of passing the time as she relaxed. She could have gone to sit with Menuzza, or could have chatted with the young girls, the oldest of whom was beginning to think of her trousseau. The child had confided to Pia, what she hadn't told her own mother, that a boy down the street had settled his choice upon her, and that she, for her part, had decided she might as well give her assent.

"You must wait," Pia had counselled in a sage but not unfriendly manner. She couldn't have told you where she had gotten the idea, but it was the advice with which she always responded to a young person's first report of love, including each of her own children's. Perhaps it grew simply from Pia's general conviction that it wasn't right to be too presumptuous in this life, to rush too eagerly towards the goals of one's heart, or even to flee too quickly from looming disaster, as if one imagined that all woe could be escaped. As to the latter, it was Pia's hope that by refusing to reveal the full extent of one's fears, one might be permitted to slip unnoticed past some of them: as if, by showing a face of calm to the doctor, you might lead him to forget that he had come to give you a shot.

At this moment, Pia had sought out the solitude of her room — it had been her parents' years ago — from a similar feeling. If she sat with Menuzza, the hair-doing over, she suspected that her niece's first words would be, "Well, so he's gone." An undeniable fact, and one not unprepared for; but just now Pia felt it would be better not to talk of it.

She didn't fear she would weep. It was sad, of course, to say goodbye, even if only for a time (she supposed he'd visit, like most emigrant husbands, once a year or so); but what novelty could there be in farewells, for a woman old as herself, that she should give way to grief? Nevertheless, Pia had a suspicion that she might cry out some sentiment — "What will I do now?" were words that came to mind — that would needlessly alarm Menuzza.

Needless it was, because in fact there was no great reason to fear the future. Although she couldn't help picturing her sons and daughters — whose faces, oddly, returned to her as they had been in childhood — she asked herself what need they could have of her now? Besides, they would come to seek her out, some day, as she herself had come. Here, fulfilling her vow, there was surely only reason to be contented.

No day need pass, for the rest of her life, when she wouldn't be free to bring fresh flowers to her mother's grave. To think of this, instead of the children — instead, even, of Nino — required some effort at first. But soon the thought so swelled her heart that she was sure it was this happiness that she had feared showing Menuzza, lest, like complimenting an infant's beauty, it draw the evil eye.

To be with her mother every day! To be far from that world of frightening things that, for all her years there, had never become familiar: that, surely, could only be a relief. To feel the very air of the town she belonged to caress her as gently as her oldest sheets, back in America. She used to patch them again and again, less for economy than for the comfort of smoothing their yearly softer fabric out again upon her bed, and imagining they would last her an eternity — though in America, to tell the truth, they didn't sew you up in your own linens. Pia stroked her hand along Menuzza's pillowcase — she had lain herself to rest for a moment — and that worn-down cloth, soft as her mother's touch upon her skin, made Pia's eyes fill up. Never to leave again, to be at peace, not for a moment, but forever: it was the tears brought by this thought, it was these tears she hadn't wanted to risk betraying to Menuzza, who would upset herself as if something were wrong.

But it seemed as if Menuzza must have guessed them, or been distressed by some other cause. For could it be anything other than distress that made her call up to her aunt's window, "Zu'Pia! Zu'Pia! Come down and see!"?

Pia wiped her eyes with the pillowcase, and smoothed her dress as she rose from the bed. Coming down the stairs, she tied her apron back on. Menuzza stood in the doorway now, beckoning her aunt to come out. She didn't look upset. She looked baffled, rather, or surprised, or amused: a complexity of feeling of the sort that could not help but trouble Pia. If even wise Menuzza didn't know what to think of what she was looking at — it was something down the street at which she glanced between times of calling her aunt — how was Pia herself to decipher it?

At last Pia was at the door, looked where Menuzza pointed, and gasped. On her face, in the next moment, might have been discerned a succession of feelings: astonishment, dismay, uncertainty, and, last of all, resignation to the fate she foresaw. It was the resignation Pia always ended by bringing, no matter with what difficulty or after what moments of despair, to all the mysteries of life. So whole-hearted was her submission, once she gave it, that it sometimes felt — as it felt now — like joy.

For she saw Nino coming down the street, in his hand, stretched toward her, something it had never held. She didn't know their name, had never known it even in her first life, when she was a child in this *paese*.

But they were flowers all the same.

Québec, Canada
1998